venu

an international literary magazine

boy girl

3

1998

Venue is published four times a year (December, March, June, September).
ISBN 90-5701-391-6
ISSN 1027-0272

Subscriptions and inquiries should be addressed to **International Publishers Distributor** in care of one of the addresses below:

P.O. Box 32160
Newark, NJ 07102 USA
Telephone: 1-800-545-8398
Fax: 973-643-7676

IPD Marketing Services
P.O. Box 310
Queen's House, Don Road
St. Helier, Jersey
Channel Islands JE4 OTH
Telephone: 44(0)118-956-0080
Fax: 44(0)118-956-8211

Kent Ridge, PO Box 1180
Singapore 911106
Republic of Singapore
Telephone: 65 741-6933
Fax: 65 741-6922

Yohan Western Publications Distribution Agency
3-14-9, Okubo, Shinjuku-ku
Tokyo 169, Japan
Telephone: 81 3 3208-0186
Fax: 81 3 3208 5308

Subscription rate:
One year (four issues):
US $38.00
GB £26.00
ECU 32.00

Trade Distribution:
Distributed Art Publishers
155 Sixth Avenue, 2nd Floor
New York, NY 10013-1507
Telephone: 212-627-1999
Fax: 212-627-9484

EDITORIAL CORRESPONDENCE:
VENUE, 151 E 25, New York, NY 10010

Unsolicited manuscripts — FICTION and ESSAYS — are welcomed. Manuscripts should be typed and double spaced and will not be returned unless accompanied by a stamped, self-addressed envelope. Submission will be taken to imply that the manuscript has never been published previously in any form and has not been simultaneously offered to any other publication. We do not accept unsolicited submissions for the FORUM.

DESIGN BY: *Terry Berkowitz*

Contents

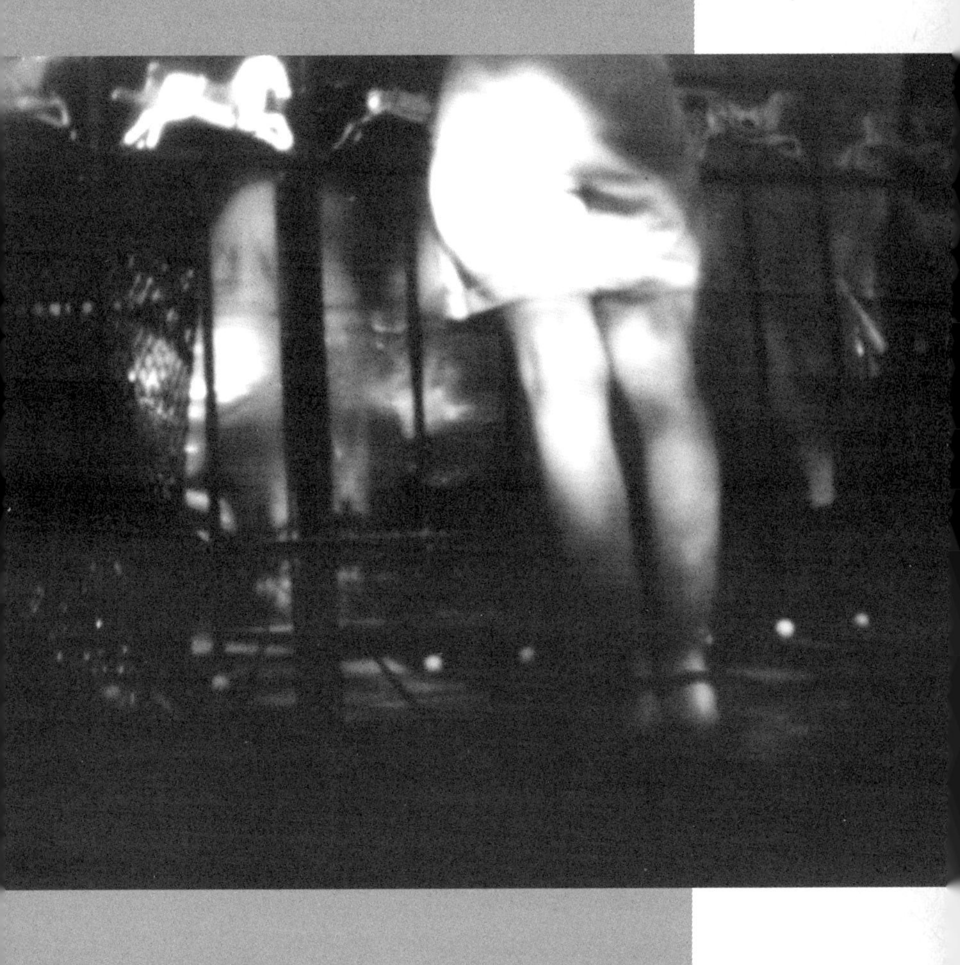

FICTION

Autobiography of an Escape Artist

Gloria Fisk

I WAS BORN IN THE MIDDLE OF A HAILSTORM, which I think is significant. The sky threw crystal exclamation points on the hospital roof to announce my arrival to the world, but in all that clatter nobody noticed me except my mother and father, who were typically young and unsuspecting. They beamed parentally and called me Lilith.

I think my name was the start of my troubles. I'm not above or below the old idea that human plots are susceptible to godly wrath, and forgiveness isn't high on Lilith's list of virtues. Taking a name strikes me as grand theft on a divine scale; gods have punished for less. Besides, my fate had to have come from somewhere. None of that ever crossed the minds of my parents though. They just liked the sound and weight of all of those consonants in the word, *Lilith*.

They brought me home and everything seemed fine for the

first few months while I crawled and gurgled like everyone does. But when falling followed standing, things changed, and the stumbles that are inherent in the experience led to more than the usual scrapes and bruises. When I crumpled into a pile on the floor, my predictable cries were accompanied by the unpredictable, undeniable sound of glass breaking. My concerned parents looked and listened, and they were mystified.

They brought me back to the doctors who had introduced me to the world, and I was examined. They exchanged murmurs and glances, collecting their data and checking it twice, since what they found was not only alarming but seemingly impossible. With clipboards in hands and furrows on brows, they leaned forward and said that somehow my skeleton was crafted out of finely blown glass.

They flew into a fury of hypotheses and publishing that was profitable for them but not for me. All I got out of it was the certainty that I would be a thing apart, a pig fetus in a jar of formaldehyde or a jewel on a satin pillow. The weeks and months that followed were a series of days laden with can'ts and shouldn'ts, since it was inevitable that as I grew the weight of me would become increasingly burdensome to the filaments I had in place of bone. I lived on a diet of rice cakes and fruit cocktail to ease the strain I felt in my hips when the occasional chocolate bar came to rest on them. To minimize the shock my feet endured when they touched the floor, I developed a shuffling way of walking, and I wore insoles for added protection.

But I wasn't unhappy. My diversions were necessarily limited, but my relations with the things and people around me were satisfying in a general if shallow way. I was an object of vague curiosity to other kids, who occasionally brought me mementos from the world they inhabited and I didn't. Once some girls gave me an old mayonnaise jar with tadpoles inside. I threw away the jar and put the tadpoles in my aquarium, where they squirmed halfheartedly for a few days before they died, and I waved gratefully back at the froggy girls from across the fine haze that surrounded me.

I felt nearly as much kinship with inanimate things as I did with living ones, and I was always aware that underneath my skin I was made of stuff that had more in common with mayonnaise jars and aquariums than with the tadpoles who lived briefly inside them. So I spent a lot of my time with objects, and grieved for the gored papers I had to staple in school.

AND I GREW UP. The things that used to seem big to me started to seem small, my frailty became fashionable, and some people thought I was beautiful. My guts started churning and I suddenly became aware of having organs. I'd sit and feel my intestines turning over and over and around themselves, sloshing inside me like laundry in a never-ending rinse cycle. It was a slightly sick feeling but I grew more attached to it every day, acquiring a taste for whiskey and raw fish and other grown-up things that are simultaneously delicious and nauseating. For the first time I had moments of wishing that the fog I lived in would lift or that someone would join me inside it.

The area around and below my stomach began to exhibit other startling qualities that became more interesting to me the more I considered them. I found that when I lay belly-down on the floor next to my stereo, I could turn the volume way up and make the reverberations pass from the speaker to the floor to me, tickling me in a way that made me crave an earthquake. The churning inside me grew more lovely by the minute, meeting the vibrations halfway and tickling them back, and I eagerly invested in a better set of speakers.

It struck me that if inanimate objects could turn the old sickness in such a positive direction, the possibilities with animate ones and their greater range of motion were endless. I began eyeing people with new interest, and they showed themselves to me in a much more flattering light. My eye fell on a boy, and I soon found myself on a couch in his basement, which is a dangerous place for a girl with glass bones to be. Above me, he reminded me of a train hurtling down the tracks, his eyes glazed over and fixed on a destination I couldn't see. Had I been less preoccupied, I might have envied him or thought of trying to join him, but all of my faculties were focused on keeping his weight off me. Even so, I winced and wiggled away as the meat around my pelvis tore against the splintering glass.

I soon decided that the world of sex with people was not for me, and my attentions drifted. I accumulated a vast treasure of vibrators and loved every one. I had antique metal Conairs that looked like farm machinery and an enormous variety of newfangled phalluses of every possible description. Some were incredibly lifelike and others reveled in their plasticness; one was patterned after a rocketship and several imitated the form and content of the human penis perfectly. I also had a lot of homemade contraptions that were full of whirring pistons and spinning wheels, with belts that sputtered and flung oil and sparks around the room day and night.

My intimacy with them made unplugged vibrators too corpselike for me to live with, so I kept them all turned on all the time. Together they hummed a low and gentle chorus like a lullaby sung by a roomful of old refrigerators, and their continuity soothed me. Besides, there was a kind of security in knowing I was never more than a few steps from guaranteed gratification with no threat of broken bones. I built a shelf for them to rest on that circled the circumference of my apartment, and my walls always throbbed faintly.

I came to life inside those walls and considered myself lucky to return to them nightly, mostly unscathed by my daily passage through the outside world. I was adept by this time at keeping it at a distance, and the years passed while I spent my days working as a word processor in a law firm. My ability to communicate with the computers on their level, coupled with the weightlessness of my marrow-free fingers, made me the most efficient and highly paid word processor in the building. The lawyers treated me with the same mixture of condescension and deference that the kids on the playground had, and I renewed my commitment to the noncommittal haziness that had kept me well liked enough to be unbothered for most of my life.

DAYS BECAME WEEKS AND YEARS, and I lived without questioning my place in things. The possibility occurred to me only rarely that the people I saw outside might actually exist in apartments too, and in all kinds of places I couldn't imagine, feeling things not only as I did but also in ways that were peculiar and private to them. This thought was too overwhelming and contrary to my experience of things for me to consider seriously, and my greatest desire from them was that they not jar my bones as they passed. Even the people I saw every day were familiar to me only in an aesthetic sense, and I acknowledged them daily just like I did the front door of my building. I turned my key in the lock with just the same consideration as I greeted the lawyers, and I got by.

But after a while, the churning feeling returned, and this time it was higher up where my vibrators were less effective. I started waking up in the middle of the night trembling from nightmares I couldn't remember, but even worse were the good dreams that stayed with me. Recurringly, I flung myself around the room, laughing as I broke every bone against tables and chairs, desks and bookcases. I jumped as high as I could, crushing my feet and legs into millions of shards embedded in flesh. When I woke up, I'd feel a tiny smile playing on my face, and I'd take a feeling of hope with me from the dream into my day.

My eyes scanned the world and assembled the range of shapes and colors disinterestedly, resting nowhere until they fell on her. She was trying on a pair of red leather gloves, slipping her hands over and around one another, admiring them. Her round shoulders wore a raincoat that looked like it had been on the floor of the closet all summer, and her eyes were circled in shadows that made me imagine her staying up all night with a sick child or a novel, and in that moment, without warning, I loved her. When I looked at the gloves embracing her hands, envy sliced through me. I wanted to be those gloves, to go away and go no place, to go home.

I went back to my apartment and filled the bathtub with water. My bones were exhausted, caving in under the weight of me, and when I sank into the tub, everything seemed to sigh as gravity loosened its hold. I floated in the water and each pore and orifice gladly opened up like a flower, pouring me out. I became the water and the water became me, and when they found me, my crystal skeleton was like so many ice cubes, bobbing and clicking lightly.

Allan Stein

Matthew Stadler

1.

This part of the thirteenth district was plain and quotidian beside the Paris I remembered from my trip with Louise. I was sixteen then and we stayed in a small hotel near the Place St. Denis, where it seemed like every street at every hour was loud and crowded, decorated with the come-hither blandishments of tourism. Car shops and overpriced cafés punctuated this twisting labyrinth of streets in every direction, and I loved it like TV: a constant, jumbled stream of pumped-up sensations that left us exhausted and irritable; so irritable that Louise and I decided for the first time in any place, traveling or at home, to go our separate ways for great chunks of time. We set up rendezvous for certain meals back at the hotel and spent the next ten days like strangers who have met each other abroad, get along well and agree to share a few dates in the course of their separate vacations. It is clear to me now that Louise, progressive mother that she was, had decided it was time I began having a sex life, some kind of life anyway, and where better for a handsome young boy to start than Paris. I know that now, but at the time of our trip what I had figured out was exactly the reverse. In Paris, thrust onto my own by my mother's eagerness to explore (as she put it), I reasoned that *she* was pursuing sex, or at least romance, and wanted to get rid of me. I was hurt by it, and suspicious. My forced independence became an affliction and I spent most of the time paranoid and morose, staying close to the hotel so I could monitor her comings and goings as closely as possible.

Our rooms were separate but they shared a thin wall and I always knew if she was in, and what she was doing when she was. Typically we had breakfast at the hotel and discussed our plans for the day. I improvised elaborate fictions, long walking tours of great swaths of the city that I never actually carried out, pinioned as I was to my surveillance of Louise. Always I had maps and guidebooks to lay over the small table, covering the coffee and stale pastries, as I explained my ambitious tours. Louise was attentive to all this bluster, but it was clear she wished I would just calm down and enjoy myself. Usually she had no plans except to go somewhere in another neighborhood and sit for a while in a café, and as I discovered, that's exactly what she did. She always invited me to come along, but since my "new independence" was the great victory of this vacation, accepting Louise's offer would clearly have been a defeat, disappointing to both of us. No, I always said, thanks, but I must get ready and be off. In my room I waited, silent for Louise to return to her room, then I scrambled out the door to an awful Formica café across from the hotel's entrance, where I had a Gini soda (in a can, no glass, so I could take it with me the moment I had to leave). I waited, hidden behind a mirrored pillar, for my mother to emerge, and then I followed her.

Louise was not a very interesting traveler. She peered in windows but rarely went inside to shop. She stopped randomly (I suppose it was usually warm sunshine that stopped her) and stood like a homeless woman for long moments doing nothing. If I lost her, which was often, it was usually in the metro where I couldn't risk sitting in the same car and had to lean out at the stops to watch the platform, hoping I would see her when she got off. I visited a great deal of Paris getting off at the wrong stop and following some other brown head through a crowd, surging along the narrow tunnels and out into the street. Stalingrad, Place de Clichy, Gare de l'Est, Mouton Duvernet and on one morning of endless mistaken tailings through three train changes, the Port de Bagnolet, where I was too exhausted to return home and spent the rest of the afternoon sitting in a sandwich shop reading a British sports newspaper. Having lost her, my usual strategy was to return to the Place St. Michel and sit in that same Formica café with an endless Gini until I saw her returning to the hotel.

In a way, I *was* beginning a sex life, as I now believe Louise had hoped; my new habit of surveillance became tremendously exciting to me, making my face flush with nervous energy, my heart race and my body become electric with that blood-rush of Eros that seems to drift so haphazardly over the hodge-podge days of adolescence — petty dinner-table arguments raising fat erections, orgasms poked, midafternoon, into television-room couch cushions, the cat or dog licking in a backyard hollow, licking just an arm, but nevertheless — and now this top-secret trailing through the streets of Paris, my erection pressed flat against my jeans, until later each afternoon in my room when I beat off. I didn't think of Louise, but of trailing her. In fact I thought mostly of myself, and while I worked my fist up and down in the dim gauze light of the hotel room what I imagined was me on the subway train, unzipping and doing it there, Louise in the next car clueless while I performed gloriously, naked for all the men and women and children in the bright enamel subway compartment to admire.

Before I could allow myself this release I sat, sometimes for hours, in the café hoping to catch her return. The man or men I thought she must be chasing never materialized, with the notable exception of one extremely handsome (thirty or forty year-old) Frenchman who had befriended both of us in the first days of our stay. His name was Frank (which sounded lovely in French with the soft "a"), and it was obvious to me he wanted to have my mother. What gave him away — beyond the touch, the attention, the body language, the great and constant amplitude of joy and strained humor, the wine, always, which he brought to our table asking could he join us — was him palling it up with me, as if *we* could be great buddies. He would show me all of Paris, everything that a boy should see. In short, he employed the trick of most men I'd seen showing interest in Louise: buddy up to the son to get mom. We enjoyed him like a fireworks display, dazzled and amused, but also very distant. He joined us for dinner three or four times and at the end of each evening, when at last Frank had withdrawn, Louise and I would just look at each other and laugh, not derisively but in amazement.

Frank had appeared twice at cafés where my mother sat, but nothing ever happened. "Appeared" is unfair, in fact Louise told me on both mornings that she was going to meet Frank who had called and wouldn't I like to come too, Frank had asked specifically for you to come, really he'll be very disappointed to see it's just this old woman, and I don't know that I'll enjoy it much without an escort, oh please, but no mother I absolutely cannot, I have the whole Buttes Chaumont to see today, not to mention the zoo of the Bois de Vincennes, which *le Guide Bleu* insists should not be missed, so that both times Louise did go "alone" and I followed with extra vigilance hoping something would at last happen. Nothing ever did. Frank seemed bored, distracted in a way quite unknown at our dinners together, and they drank their coffees, chatted for less than an hour, kissed cheek-cheek, and I returned to the hotel to beat off.

ON THE SEVENTH DAY, AT LAST, something happened. I had lost her one morning in the metro going north from St. Michel and returned to the tacky café where I found an American newspaper and parked myself in the best spot, facing a mirrored wall which caught the hotel entrance in its dulled and greasy panorama. I could read and watch at the same time from there. I was only mildly bored, halfway through a canned Gini, when I spotted Frank standing by the hotel door looking at his watch. So, it had come to this — clandestine rendezvous while the boy hiked the Canal de l'Ouro out to view the modern treasure of the Parc La Villette. All the dreary hours spent in this bright orange café, scraping the flimsy feet of my plastic chair across the tiles, all of my week in Paris spent day-after-day in this ugly hole waiting, suddenly became worthwhile, like hot bread in the hands of a starving man. I dropped the paper and tore ravenously out the clattering glass door, Gini in hand, to intercept this desirous *paramour* before he could have his way with my mother.

"Hey," I called, feigning enthusiasm, rushing up to Frank.

"Oh, hello." From him a flash of true distress, with a smile propped up quickly in its wake. "What a great surprise."

"Waiting for someone?" I managed to say, not coy at all, and I sipped the Gini, to hide the pleasure of my trap.

"I'm not sure. I mean I have no appointment with anyone, if that's what you ask. I'm awfully glad to see you."

Uh-huh. "Yeah, what a coincidence."

"Not so much of one, really, I know this is your hotel." Horribly, I thought he might try now to confide their rendezvous to me, the man-to-man ploy, demanding my confederacy, and I forestalled him with a quick invitation.

"Come up to my room, Frank, you've never seen it have you?" If I could get him in there for long enough, Louise wouldn't find him, and there would be no rendezvous.

"If you want me to," he answered ambiguously. I was silent, petulant and impatient to get out of there.

"Whatever," I said, hurrying into the lobby, drawing him along in my wake. "Come on." Frank looked around anxiously, a last scan for dear late Louise, then he followed me inside.

The charm came back on. Frank smiled now, positively aglow once we got in the elevator. He really could turn it on, and I supposed he was revving the engines to get this whole distraction up and running and over with quick enough to catch his real date. As it turned out, that wasn't the case at all. Frank put his hand on my shoulder as I turned the key, and when we pushed through the door he slammed it closed behind us and pinned me to the wall of the tiny room. He pulled the buttons of my shirt undone one-by-one while kissing me flat on the mouth. His tongue found my lips, parted in complete surprise, before pushing past them. My mind went everywhere while my body went definitely one way only and that was all over Frank. Regardless of what I thought (and I thought nearly everything) my belly and chest pushed toward him and my erection pressed at the metal buttons of my jeans. He pried them undone and pulled my pants down my legs. Was I beautiful? What boy is not beautiful? Frank dragged my underpants off, a dirty frayed pair, grabbing and tugging so I got burns along my hips, and then he fell on me. I felt my life come rushing down through the top of my head, along my spine and then, after a span in which he bit me and pinched my nipples until they were sore and raw, it all burst out my middle and into his mouth. And then I slapped him, hard across the face, which amazed and delighted me. I don't know if or when Louise returned, I don't think she did until after dinner, but Frank and I had sex every day for the next three days, and then I left Paris. Sex was terrific, but Frank never acted affectionate before or after it, and that was fine. It meant I didn't fall in love at all. After we left I hardly thought about him, except when I beat off and would replay the scene in the hotel room. I still do. It's one of my favorite scenes.

2.

Perhaps you don't see the boy in close detail, notice the pitch of pant, soft nape of the neck, nor the slight pulse of blood in the arteries of his throat. At the risk of exhausting you, I'll just provide a cursory tour. Dogan's feet in stylish low-top sneakers, the suede sort favored by skateboard boys, were elegant and long, aristocratic, with a high arch and a gentle laxness in the joints. When he pulled the baggy legs of his beaten blue jeans up only a casual few inches to scratch an ankle or two, thick droopy socks of white cotton were seen resting in folds against the soft rims of his shoes. The ankle, bared for scratching, was smooth, tan, olive-skinned actually, and pronounced, with soft golden hair ceasing abruptly along a stirrup-shaped border just above the knob. It would be pleasing to press one's nose there, both to feel the ticklish hairs and to smell the warm odor of the boy's long legs. Inside the jeans you can only imagine, or I recreate from memory, the French curve of his calves leading to simple knees whose greatest features were the hollows behind them: soft, deep as eggs, warm and bordered by the firm stretch of twin tendons from the lower thighs, there where the muscle connected to the backs of the knees. I kept my nose here when I could, which meant my eyes, forehead and pleasing shock of hair were pressed to the broad, hamlike expanse of the backs of his thighs (no hair here but mine). Reaching around the front to fiddle, I was continually impressed by the great haunches of meat this lithe boy stored in his long legs. Soccer, I supposed. His bottom, too, was smooth and rounded and, to return to your perspective, kept the baggy jeans perched at a delicious tilt, so that the loosely belted waist, while oversized enough to fit two hands snugly down the front (usually his, resting and caressing), rode the back upper midbutt serenely, bordered all around by a brilliant billow of flannel boxer shorts. The fly, with its battered, dented buttons half-loosened from their nooks, was always puckered where his languorous organ pushed and nudged. When he stood, you could see it, breathing and sighing behind the folds of distressed fabric, and it was pleasure to stand *en face* and press the flattened palm of one hand against the pucker of his fly, which press was returned from within, amplified. Are we only to the waist? Dogan wore a shirt on this winter evening in the Grand Marble Bar, baggy and striped with fatigue-green and auburn, but surely everyone has seen the boy shirtless, and in the grand array of life's exertions: half-stripped and sweating at work in the shop stacking boxes; speeding down the left wing in his wind-torn shorts chasing World Cup dreams; emerging from the pool all arms and gangly legs, dewdropped and shivering; or asleep in the shade of a summer tree, shorts askew, drooling on the pried-open pages of his required reading. I'm sure you recall the dizzying vertigo, running your eyes along the tattered waistband riding so low and loose off twin-ridged hips it seemed whole religions could be founded in the space between that drifting lip of cotton and his trim, shallow bellybutton. I'd like to stroll along the rim, tasting the rounded flat of belly that stretches out from its spiral origin there, driving hands across the broad flat plain, dusky horizons distant on either side, and the promise of shelter in the shadowed hollows south where the landscape becomes variegated and interesting. But we've been there. So *up* along the sides of his slim torso (alarming how thin he is where the hips give in, so small you feel you could wrap two hands around him, twin thumbs pressed into his bellybutton, and have fingertips touch on the other side) up the knobby-ridged ribs moving visibly as he breathes. Dogan ran his mindless hands over his ribs, up to fold the soft nipple, then back down to the hips, always, when he stood shirtless talking. His shoulder blades were delicate and pronounced. They moved like angel's wings when he moved. Many days could be spent between them, in the parallel grooves of his spine, feathering outward along his ribs or leaning into the uncaged flanks below. Lying on his stomach he enjoyed my two hands on his hips rocking his weight back and forth so that he made love to the blanket he lay on. And then my one hand slipped in between his slightly parted legs and pushed upward, under. We liked that too. Above, face front, where his ribs converged, a singular divot, pulsing with the exertions of his heart, invited my tongue to rest. He smelled like sweet milk and dust where my nose then pressed, hard against the plate of bone his taut skin hid. Turning my head to either side, the slightest rise of muscle defined all of my horizons and led to nipples I have already described (supple and thin as rose petals when warm and taut if pulled on, cold or agitated, I think it was). A boy can caress his nipples, entertaining an idle hand, or share them with a friend bumping chests or lying pressed side to side, without censure. His shirt this evening was large enough (pulled and stretched around the collar) to reveal the shadowed hollows of his collarbones plus shoulders as slim as they were rounded and beautiful (punctuated with knobs and muscles that echoed the harmony of his calves and ankles). A delicate necklace of flat, linked gold lay along his throat like sleep. I enjoyed Dogan's long arms, especially the surprise of what he could reach, even when I was on my knees in front of him. You could easily wrap your hands around his little throat and squeeze. The veins and striations, everything vital, was pressed to the surface there. I spent long spent minutes exhausted (we were always in a hurry, after) watching the decelerating trill of his carotid artery animate that thin neck. This artery was taut and pressured, dwarfed by its neighbor, the restless Adam's apple. From the billowing short sleeves of his skater-tee in the Grand Marble Bar, his arms dangled, angular and elegant, as he fiddled with his pants cuff. A filthy braided twine was tied loosely around one wrist, which it never left. I cannot capture the weak beauty of his wrists. I imagine them crushed in the jaws of an industrial menace, or motionless amongst the ferns of a brook in the springtime woods where the boy has drowned. In either case the wrists beg to be touched, their knobs caressed as the last pulse of blood plunges through the soft underside where the veins are. I read in the news about a man who murdered boys, and on the eve of his execution he said "everyone thinks this is the end, that it's all over now. But where do you think I came from?" Murder may simply be a more extreme form of love or description, but what keeps me from it is the deep embarrassment, shame even, that I would feel for doing something so pig-headed and final. That is what I was thinking in any case. Who knows what the boy thought? His face I will describe later.

3.

We arrived at noon and left our bags with a woman who said she worked for the hotel. There was no one else on the platform when the train pulled away, only this stout, very serious woman, some complacent mongrel edging along a ditch sniffing for scraps, plus me and the boy. She had a pushcart littered with dried flowers and we put our bags on that. The hotel turned out to be more of a ruin, really, than a hotel, but she couldn't very well have said hello, let me take your bags, I work for the ruin. Off she went, with the flowers and the bags, down the one narrow road toward town.

I was lightheaded from the air which was breezy and, after two days of freakish winter snow without proper mittens or what-have-you, at last springlike and warm. Ocean and pine and dust mixed with heady currents of mimosa and the fresh iodine tang of seaweed left stranded on the rocks by an outgoing tide. The boy stared at the sea, probably exhausted by his fever and my having kept him up all night with the cool washcloth and the wine. It was unnaturally beautiful. Red, crenelated rock broke from the scruffy pine headlands, crumbling toward the sea, carpeted in patches with lavender, rosemary and scrub brush. The sea was blue like metal. Where it touched the rock there was no blending, just the sharp brick-red rock against the cold metal sea. The strand of beach between the rigid headlands was white, the sand imported from some other shore so that it looked false, like a fancy ribbon or prize strung across the flushed bosom of a very determined farm girl. (I remember her standing in a meadow of bluebells, this particular girl — not a farm girl at all really as it is my mother I am recalling, whose image was suggested by the falseness of the beach at Agay — sunshine raking the steep, wooded hills that bordered "our" meadow, and a goat she taunted to rage so that she might show me how to vault over the animal as it charged, placing her two hands on the nubs of its horns, her legs in an elegant "V" sailing over the befuddled goat whose violence turned to distraction when the target disappeared. The sea was visible there too, which is maybe why I thought of her.)

I will list the features of this final vista the boy and I shared: the disappearing train, a slinky metal worm, crawling along the edge of the rocks until it vanished beyond the third headland; small groves of plum trees in the broad, shadowed canyon carved by the river on its course from the hills to the sea; that woman with the flower cart, distant but still visible, pausing to shake dirt from her shoe, on her way through town to the hotel; signs, in French of course, pointing one way to "Agay, Cannes, Nice" and the other to "St. Raphael, Marseille"; a calendar (notice how neatly these details triangulate our location) which was unreadable, obscured by distance and the warped glass of the stationmaster's office window; the boy's face (this my view), pale from sickness, but utterly enchanting still, the wide gap between his rabbit teeth, small even nose and brown eyes just slightly too close, so that I kept focusing on the corners where they teared, a rounded chin and big mouth so soft he looked like he might still be suckling (he was fifteen); long dirty sand-colored hair, dull and stringy, pushed behind his wide blushing ears. The noon sun raised a painful glare off the platform and the boy put on dark glasses which made him look like a pop star. The sky was squashed and bruised blue. To the south, beyond the sea's curving horizon (Africa down there), distance sucked all order from the sky and left it washed out and miasmic.

There is not an hour of my life I do not see this vista obscured by signposts, around a corner, through trees, on a wrong turn past the ferry dock, or while scrambling to the edge of a sand cliff that is crumbling in the waves of another sea. I smell it in the scattering swirl of snow around an open-windowed car driving through the mountains, or on a crowded tram in some foreign city whose park has just opened its scrubbed, pale gardens of rosemary and gravel and lavender. It billows and collapses this perpetual memory, continually verging on the real. The tram, my stop and all of the day's good intentions can be swallowed in the momentary rupture this constantly returning spectacle creates. In that breathless gap, marked by my revery, space collapses into nothing and at the same time enlarges to monstrous, devouring proportions — rather like the panoramic view of a reader with his nose buried in a book. The world shuts down around him, and everything, thereby, opens up.

The boy went to the wall of the stationmaster's office and sat on a slatted bench in the shade. He was still feverish and standing in the sun made him dizzy. I had his blue knapsack with the bottled water and I offered it to him. The hum and the clatter of the rails, transmitting the train's prolonged departure, diminished to nothing. Insects could be heard, together with the waves collapsing on the shore below us. The breeze made a huffing sort of dull whistle through the station's entrance where there was no door to prevent it. The boy spoke English when it suited him, but just now he understood nothing, neither the word "water" nor the obvious gesture I made with the bottle itself. He stared past me, looking puzzled.

ADULTS, SO CRUEL, CAN BE AMUSED in the face of a child's suffering. Even while we comfort him a part of us can be laughing at, for example, a hurt boy's exaggerated pout. This doesn't compromise our sympathy, it's just amusing in a way that the boy can't possibly understand. It can't be explained to his satisfaction. When I cried my mother used to laugh out loud with pleasure, and weep at the same time, while holding me. Her laughter was baffling and upsetting, like cruelty, and it made me cry all the more, which prolonged both the laughter and the embrace until in the end we were both just exhausted and sobbing, holding onto each other, having said nothing. I was not so cruel to the boy, but that was because I loved him and because my mother's cruelty had taught me not to be.

I have loved boys even when they despised me. This boy did not despise me, but that is perhaps because we had little in common. In the garden he picked flowers and taught me to name them in French, but I quickly forgot all the names. I could only remember what his mouth looked like as he said them. What else do I recall? His bare hips, delicately turned as he lay in bed beside me. A glimmer of sweat limning the hollow of his back. Night, its gradual onset, and then our long slow recline. The boy (he was French, fifteen, as I've said, and he believed I could deliver him from a humdrum life and family which had begun to seem tedious and doomed) turned to me across the bunched pillows and let his soft chin rest on my shoulder. His nipples had softened and lay flat. His skin was warm from an increasing fever. I think it's okay for you to take pleasure in these things. He took my hand in his and drew it along his ribs to his belly and hip, and then he let my fingers touch the perfect lip of his shallow bellybutton, where I stopped for a moment to dwell.

His name is not important. I have called him, at one time or another, noodle boy, *le beau scout*, Blaise, Tony, your nipples are delicate as cherry blossoms, Miss Pants, my pal, *bougie*, M Steve, Mister Sister, *l'escalier*, *garçon vérité*, thrush or dove, Dogan, bastard, son of a bitch, kike, jew-boy, death-star-in-pants, my White House ultimate love, Aki, anodyne, Alex, Rex and Allan, but his given name was Stéphane. I lived with his family in Paris for two weeks before the events which brought us to the seaside ruin, and I'm certain they would be horrified by my story. I loved Stéphane, I might have already mentioned that. Though my account will lapse into coarseness, flippancy, lies and pure pornography, you must never forget that I truly and impossibly did love him. I lived with his family under a false pretense (which I will tell you about shortly), but we became friends and only the mother blames me for what happened to their son.

MY STORY BEGAN PROPERLY in the perpetual darkness of last winter (almost spring, it was March) in the city where I used to live. Typically I woke up in the dark, 6:00 a.m. on most days, delivered from sleep by the icy stream of air spilling in my open window. The lit clock of the railroad tower said 6:00 exactly. This round clock of black iron and creamy glass was the first thing I saw in the mornings. I would unlatch the window and push it up to let the air in. No one was ever on their way to work yet, nor had the lumbering buses and trucks started with their tentative, practice engine-roars. (Later, in clouds suffused with the bright yellow and opium-poppy-orange of the risen sun they would billow in every district of the city like grim flowers and release their belched gray emissions, which gave a pleasant taste to the winter air.) I am a teacher, or had been, which explains the early hour.

Opening the window from bed, only my head and one arm untucked, was my first habit of the morning. It was independent of me, like shifting the buried, cool pillows to the top in the deep middle of the night, neither conscious nor strictly unconscious — something between a dream and the address of a friend (which I had scribbled while dragging the phone as near to the table as it would go before absently tossing the newspaper on which I had written it into the garbage along with the bones of a fish, so that it was lost both there and in my mind until, when the brisk air of morning rushed in the open window, the whole address, neatly printed, leapt to view, bright and clear as the pinpoint stars, noisy as a child, and my mind's eye, conscious, grasped it again, though only for a moment). Minutes later, in the chaos of morning, it was gone, but so was any consciousness of having lost it.

All my thoughts were thin and brittle when I woke. My expansive dreams, ideas which multiplied like the crystalline spread of urine released into space (which I have heard is a beautiful sight, witnessed only by astronauts, the discharge turning golden and immense in the black void), became whole great cities of geometrical fantasy, complex and beautiful as hoarfrost, before shattering suddenly into unreadable shards at the slightest touch of fact or feeling (a crease in the pillow bothering my cheek, for example, or the sour taste scraped from my teeth by a dull, swollen tongue). The scrim of night outside was fragile. Its black mask could not hide the sheer abundance of the day ahead, nor the fact that it was morning already elsewhere, evening again elsewhere still and a bright summer afternoon somewhere so distant one passed through two accelerated days in the metal shell of a jet airplane just to get there. Louise once asked me what separates one place from another. I was only a child, and of course I had no idea. Other places, I guessed, which begged the question.

The oatmeal I ate before bed and left too close to the coiled heater was covered by a film of dry skin which burst under the slightest pressure, my thumb, for example, if it strayed too deeply gripping the bowl which I carried in one hand to the dirty porcelain sink. I always licked this thumb, after its plunge, and the cold sweet paste it unearthed from beneath the film was enjoyable. I could hear my friend Herbert, in the adjacent apartment, bellowing fragments of popular songs, which he only ever partly remembered. Herbert and I were always awake early, even while the rest of the city slept. He is the curator of the city's art museum, and they let him keep whatever hours he likes. I had no reason to be awake. The school where I taught resolved some misgivings that arose over Christmas by granting me a paid leave of absence.

I was accused of having sex with a tenth-grader in late December. This student, Dogan, was Turkish, lithe and very beautiful. I have a picture of him here on my wall. I tutored him on Saturdays in his apartment after his soccer practice, but I had never imagined molesting him until the principal suggested it by notifying me of the charges. Amidst the dust and gadgetry of the principal's meticulous office, his chair overburdened by the abundance he had squeezed onto its cupped seat, "had sex with the boy" floating in the well-lit air between us, my mind produced the following scenario (new to me):

On Saturday I arrive early. Dogan has showered after soccer and water dapples the bare skin of his shoulders and chest. He's wearing shorts, drinking a soda when I get there, drying his wet hair with a towel. His lips and nipples enchant me. They have similar skin, rosy and supple, thinner and more tender than the olive skin around them. "Let's get started," I tell him. He takes the book and I stand behind his chair as he settles. "Read the first poem out loud." It is García Lorca. I put my hands on his shoulders as he reads.

"No one understood the perfume of your belly's dark magnolia."

"Do you know the word 'magnolia'?" Both my hands slip over his rounded shoulders, so that my fingers reach his nipples. He keeps still.

"Magnolia is like a tree or a bush, right?"

"Yes, and a flower. Keep going."

"No one knew you tormenting love's hummingbird between your teeth. A thousand Persian ponies fell asleep in the moonlit plaza of your forehead." Here he stops and I'm worried he will get up, but he stays still. "Hmmm, forehead." It's the imagery, not my seduction, that has him bothered. "As four nights through I hugged your waist, snow's enemy." He slouches further into the chair as he reads, almost lying there, and I see his shorts tent and then relax. I move both hands over his ribs, then back up, pinching his nipples when he gets to the line about his waist. He is so slim I can feel his heart moving in the skin beneath my hand. If he didn't want it I wouldn't do it, I think I'm thinking.

"Those words should all be quite clear," I say. "Just continue."

"Between plaster and jasmines your glance was a pale seed branch." He holds the book in one hand and pulls the waistband of his shorts down along his hip with the other. His thigh is pale where he has exposed it. I slide my hand over his belly and into his shorts and he drops the book. His penis is very shapely, curving up onto his belly and it's big enough to fill my hands. The glans of his penis has the same pink skin as his nipples and lips. I kneel between his legs and put it into my mouth. I pull it out and stroke the shaft and the head, pushing it around to inspect it. Dogan is tipped back in the chair with his hands entwined behind his head. His underarms are pale and hairless.

I tell him, "Lorca's poem might appear to be unreal, but its dreamlike consistency can supplant waking reality by the force of a new coherence and logic, so that one becomes lost in it, like in fantasy or sleep, and the logical yardsticks of waking life that make its measure false are completely lost from view."

"Finish," he says, pouting. He bumps his thighs against my face, and I finish the blowjob.

SO YOU CAN IMAGINE THE DIFFICULTY I had denying the principal's charges. Why *hadn't* I molested the boy? For no good reason I could find, except maybe a failure of the imagination. The fact I had done nothing seemed to be a mere accident of timing.

"I've never had sex with him," I said in my defense.

"I believe you," our fidgety principal replied (and I believed that he did believe). "I know that you haven't done anything, the difficulty is proving it."

"What did the boy say happened?"

"Oh, he didn't say anything. His parents have accused you. They think he's covering it up because he likes it." He likes it? I was buoyed by this news, relieved to hear that my advances were welcome (never mind that there had been no advances, and no response and no victim, whose approval would still have been mere parental rumor).

"That's a relief."

"What is?"

"Nothing." Only minutes after hearing the accusation I was already planning a seduction. I cannot exaggerate how subtle and profound these chameleon confusions were. Placed at the scene of a multi-car accident I might become Florence Nightingale or a competent policeman directing worried traffic past the pools of blood and metal. At a boxing match, I have no doubt, I would thirst for the most horrifying results.

I pursued him. In the end I succeeded in committing the crime I had been falsely accused of. The parents never found me out (no one did). As it turned out, sex was precisely what the boy wanted, and he became very much the happy, satisfied child they hoped he would be, where before, during the months that I was blind to him, he had been miserable and distracted (precisely the condition, noticed by his parents, which led to the accusation that I was molesting him). In light of the boy's satisfaction, and the handsome salary I was then receiving for a great expanse of free time in which it became that much easier to meet him, clandestinely, for sex, I must admit that sometimes the whole horrifying affair became ironic and laughable. After a while he grew bored or ashamed and stopped seeing me.

Herbert was the only friend I discussed this with. Others, especially my colleagues from school, were so moved by the weight of the "tragic accusations" that I could feel myself *becoming* tragic simply with the approach of their cloying, caring glances. Their eyes had the gleam and submerged instability of glaciers, vast sheets of luminous ice beneath which chasms creaked and yawned. One would appear uninvited before my table at a café, fat Mr. Stack the math teacher, for example, and shuffle toward me as if compelled by this hollowness behind his eyes, as slow and devouring as the ice that once crawled down the face of the continent. (My mother once described a boyfriend of hers this way, one evening while she and I sat at a diner eating hot turkey sandwiches, with gravy, a special treat she gave me far more often than I deserved. It wasn't five minutes before this very boyfriend appeared at the window with his face to the glass, miming hello and making a fool of himself. She winked at me, then looked right past him blowing smoke from her cigarette, saying nothing. Finally he went away.) I just avoided my colleagues when I could or, if forced by good manners to accept a repeated invitation to lunch, tried to speak cheerfully about the fictions I devised, which, like most lies, eventually became true. I have none of my mother's cold reserve. V

These three excerpts are from the novel ALLAN STEIN, *which Grove Press is publishing.*

The One Facing Us

Ronit Matalon

1.

He married her for her papers. Did you know that's why he married her, Julien?" the niece asks with her mouth full, dunking her *tartine* in a bowl of coffee.

"Everyone knows," Julien says. He is bent over the dishwasher, the upper half of his body naked. He has worked for the Sicourelles for six years, since he was seventeen. "Everyone envies me because of Julien," Madame Sicourelle complains. "Madame de Vilalville has tried to steal him from me more than once."

"Has she really?" the niece asks with interest.

"Yes," Julien says with a smile, baring his white teeth.

"That pleases you," she observes as she fishes a piece of bread out of the bowl and wipes her fingers on the silk bathrobe Madame Sicourelle just gave her.

"Surprise!" she had announced from the foyer, tossing her keys on the table. "Surprise!" The niece had been lying on the couch, watching a game show on television, occasionally extending her arm toward a bowl of lemon candies. "Surprise, Esther, did you hear me?" She placed a large shiny package on the niece's knees. "Open it."

"What is it?"

"Open it, open it, it's something you need."

The niece smoothed the silky purple fabric against her chest. "This is something I need?"

"Every woman needs a *robe de chambre* — at least one good one. Guests come, people stop by, you never know who's going to show up. This way you're prepared."

"Nobody stops by in the morning. Who stops by in the morning?"

"Don't split hairs, Esther. Besides, you know very well that Richard sometimes brings something to your uncle, or Erouan comes in. People stop by."

Esther tried on the robe, tying the long belt high under her breasts and turning around. "I've never had a robe like this."

"Come here," Madame ordered, pursing her lips in thought. She undid the belt and tied it again, this time around Esther's waist. "Here, like this. You don't want to look like someone who's just gotten out of an institution."

They heard the clatter of Erouan's keys landing on the table next to Madame's. He came in exuding cologne and engine grease, kissing their cheeks eight times, four kisses each. "Did you just get up now?" He surveyed Esther in amazement.

"I bought her a new robe," Madame explained. "What do you think of her in the new robe?"

He narrowed his eyes. "Fine, a bit long. Isn't it a little long?"

"It's a robe, Fufu, not a dress made to order. A robe needs to be a little long and a little wide so that it's comfortable," Madame Sicourelle insisted.

"She'll step on it, Maman. She'll be wiping the floor with it."

Esther took the robe off, tried to fold it carefully and gave up, placing it in a heap in the wrapping. "It's all right. I doubt I'll wear it much anyway."

"Why not?" Madame Sicourelle lit a cigarette, waving the match in the air long after it had gone out. "Why wouldn't you wear it, Esther?"

"I don't know. It's for a lady — I'd feel ridiculous."

Madame Sicourelle stubbed out the cigarette in an ashtray. The reddish folds of her neck hung limply under her chin like a wattle, suddenly very obvious. "I'm going to rest for a while," she said.

Erouan poured himself something to drink and sat down beside Esther on the couch. They watched the game show. In an apron wrapped twice around his slim, bony waist, Augustin bustled about them incessantly, plumping up pillows, moving vases and china and brass objects from place to place. "I think I insulted her," the niece said.

"Maman is just tired. Don't pay any attention."

"She was angry at me, I'm sure of it."

"Don't be ridiculous."

"Didn't you notice her mood suddenly changed?"

"No."

He gulped down the rest of his drink and went to pour another. The niece looked at him contemptuously. His pants hung low on his hips, just barely clearing his flat backside. His wallet poked out from his back pocket. "How could you not notice that her mood changed?"

He came back and sat down on the sofa, two pillows away from her. He stared at the television screen. "He won a car, that guy." The large man in a diamond-patterned nylon shirt put his foot on the car's bumper, clapping his hands at the applauding audience. Erouan's eyelids dropped heavily, fluttered open for an instant, then dropped again. The niece turned the television off, got up and straightened the pillows. "What are you doing?" Erouan asked, startled, rubbing his cheeks.

"Just tidying up a bit."

"Leave it. Augustin will do it later."

"Augustin is going home soon. It's almost five."

"So he'll do it tomorrow," he said with a shrug, stretching his arms and yawning. "I'm beat."

His face was pasty beneath the blue and red capillaries that formed a tangled network across his cheeks, the traces of too much drink and too much sleep. "Why are you beat, Erouan?" she asked.

"What did you say?"

"I asked why you're so beat. What have you been doing?"

"I was on the boat all day. The mechanic was supposed to come but he didn't show."

"Ah."

He paused. "I can take you out some time if you like."

"When?"

"One of these days, when it isn't too hot."

"It's always too hot."

"But some days are worse than others."

"Are they?" she asked, pulling the skin under her eyes toward her cheeks, revealing the red rims of her eyes.

"HE'S SLIPPERY. YOU FEEL LIKE YOU'RE SLIDING down a wall whenever you talk to him," she tells Julien the next morning in the kitchen. Julien is slicing purplish onions, barely moving his rounded shoulders, shiny brown as if they had been rubbed with oil; only his wrists rise and fall in a steady rhythm.

"Mademoiselle does not like Monsieur Erouan," he says.

The onions make her eyes tear. "It's not that I don't like him, I just don't understand how his mind works."

He slides the thin onion rings into a pot. "She left him without taking a thing," Julien says, "just the shirt on her back. She went back to France."

"Who?"

"Dominique. His wife. Poor Monsieur Erouan."

Esther twirls some hair around her finger. "I didn't know he had a wife."

Julien turns back to the gas burners, flinching slightly at a spray of hot oil. "Mademoiselle does not know many things."

She is standing beside him, watching the onion rings turn golden in the pot. "Like what, for instance?" His arm, stirring vigorously, brushes against hers. Two thick droplets of sweat hang quivering from his left nipple, which is pink against the magnificent brown chest.

"Be careful of the oil, Mademoiselle," he says, lightly brushing her hand away from where it rests on the counter.

Her hand reaches for his long, damp neck. "Don't move, Julien."

He shuts his eyes. "*Ne bouge pas*," the niece says. Her fingers fan out over the width of his nape, her pinky edging toward his bristly, shaven hairline. He drops his head back, mouth open, eyes closed, rubbing against her palm. The hand that holds the spoon is frozen in mid-air. Esther sees their reflection in the panes of the kitchen window: two heads, one upright silhouette, drowning in the broad outline of a tree visible from the other side, from the garden. A car door slams in the distance. "Madame has come back," Julien says flatly without moving his head, without opening his eyes.

Julien has a nephew who is active in an underground movement agitating against the government of Cameroon. The nephew does not have a job. He sits for hours on a large rock by the gate near Augustin's hut, his head resting on his knees, dozing and waiting for Julien to finish work. Julien brings him food and sometimes alcohol in an empty oil bottle. The nephew's name is François.

"Why don't you get a job sometime, François?" Julien chides him.

The nephew teases him back. "Right away, boy. Right this minute, boy," he says, imitating Madame Sicourelle. Sometimes Julien shoos him away but he always shows up again, sharing secrets with the elderly Augustin, who scratches his chin in amazement.

"Why is François always making trouble? Cameroon is independent," the niece says now, trying to keep her voice casual.

"Begging your pardon, Mademoiselle, but you simply do not understand what is happening to our country," Julien says. "Everything here is corrupt. Everything."

"And François and his friends will suddenly make everything not corrupt?"

Julien has begun scrubbing a copper pot with lemon and steel wool, his breath rising and falling. "François says we shouldn't sleep with white women."

Esther straightens her glasses. "You're not sleeping with me."

"No, but it's like that."

"It isn't. You can tell your cousin not to worry."

"He's my nephew."

"Nephew, cousin, whatever. Maybe he's just projecting his own fantasies."

Julien's arm jerks away from the pot and he places the ball of steel wool in Esther's hand. He closes his fist over hers and squeezes hard. Beads of sweat fall from his forehead. Madame Sicourelle is out in the garden, giving instructions in a loud voice. After a minute Julien lets go and Esther's palm is scored with bloody scratches. She pats at her hand with a kitchen towel before Julien dips it into a bowl of tepid water, shaking her wrist lightly. Her slack fingers trace circles in the water. Cupping his own hand, Julien collects some water and pours it over his face, neck and chest. He kneels at the niece's feet and the streams of water wet the thin cloth of her dress as it clings to her thighs. "You shouldn't have done that but I forgive you," the niece says, rubbing water over his feverish shoulders, neck and lips.

Julien opens bloodshot eyes. "Who are you, Mademoiselle, to forgive me?"

ESTHER AVOIDS THE KITCHEN FOR TWO WEEKS. She watches Julien from the windows of her room, which face the wide kitchen window. His black shadow is blurred behind the linen screens. He moves silently, sometimes facing the window. "You've stopped sitting in the kitchen," Madame Sicourelle notes. The niece is reading; she moistens a fingertip with her tongue and turns the page. "I'm glad you've stopped sitting there."

"Why?"

"It simply isn't done. One doesn't talk to the help."

"Because they're black?"

"First of all because they're servants."

"But also because they're black."

"If you wish, yes, also because of that. Everyone is talking about Monsieur Sicourelle's niece who sits with the boy for hours."

"What else are they saying?"

"I don't know what they gossip about, but give them a chance and they'll spread all sorts of lies. Madame de Karini's boy said it. She overheard him."

The niece sits up and throws the book to the floor, her hands shaking. "What do you care what this one says or that one says? What do you care about all of this...this talk. It's racism, just plain racism." Eyes brimming, she runs to her room, dragging a small rug that gets caught in the buckle of her sandal. She shakes it free in a rage, then slams the door. Half an hour later, Madame Sicourelle knocks. "Esther," she calls softly. "Open the door, Esther." She waits a few minutes, then knocks again. "You needn't take it so personally. Please, I'm asking you."

In the evening the uncle returns, limping. He sprained his ankle going down the stairs, twisted something. Julien brings him a small footstool for the injured leg and sets the table for supper. "Where is she?" asks the uncle.

"She's been in her room all afternoon," Madame tells him. "She won't open the door for anyone, imagine that."

"What happened?"

"How should I know? She was hurt that I told her not to sit in the kitchen so much."

"Why did you say such a thing to her?" he says, kicking the stool aside. "Why do you pester her with your pettiness, tell me?" He limps to the door of her room, knocks forcefully. "Esther, do you hear me?" She comes out.

"I'm not very hungry, *mon oncle*."

He pulls her by the arm into the kitchen. "You want to be in the kitchen? We'll be in the kitchen. Julien, set the table here." Julien puts on his white waiter's jacket with the two deep pockets in front, padding silently on bare feet, moving among the three of them with a silver tray laden with baked potatoes and roast beef. Madame doesn't utter a peep.

An hour after the meal Julien is in the kitchen scrubbing tiles and the fronts of kitchen cupboards. Monsieur and Madame Sicourelle doze in front of the television in the living room. The niece returns to the kitchen to pour herself some cold water. "Are you still here?"

Julien wrings out the rag in the sink. "You know I am,

Mademoiselle."

She watches his long fingers twist the rag. "Julien," she begins, then falls silent. He turns his face toward her from the sink. It has the terrible pallor of fatigue, a pallor that seems to collect in the lips. "A baby was born to me yesterday," he says. "A son."

"Congratulations, Julien."

"Thank you, Mademoiselle."

"Is it your first?"

"He is the first."

"Well." She leaves, only to come back seconds later. "I forgot my water."

"It's not so cold anymore. Shall I pour you some fresh water?"

"That's okay, I'll take this. Thank you, Julien."

SHE SINKS INTO ONE OF THE EASY CHAIRS on the porch, smoking and listening to the noises from the road beyond the trees. A shrill screech pierces her eardrums. She walks toward the sound, looking up at the tangled treetops. "Strange bird," she says aloud. A wide ditch near Augustin's hut is dark and lumpy, smelling of good, fecund soil. Simon, the gardener, has stuck a hoe in the ditch and left it there. Esther sits, leaning against a tree trunk, her knees to her chest. She is careful to keep her body within the confines of the circular shadow cast by the tree. Soft feline steps move down the path: Julien is going home, the plastic bag with his work clothes rustling. The niece looks away from the path. Branches move and dry leaves crackle with a pleasing, spine-tingling sound.

"Are you there, Mademoiselle?"

From the corner of her eye she can see the hem of his pants and the soles of his feet in rubber flip-flops. "Yes. I'm all right, Julien."

"Are you crying, Mademoiselle?"

"I'm not crying, I'm just a little tired and upset, that's all."

"You're not used to this."

"What am I not used to?"

"The way people behave here. You're not used to it."

"Lucky me." She wipes her nose.

He stands on tiptoe and plucks a mango from a high branch. "It has a large pit but it's tasty," Julien says. "Shall I peel it for you?"

She shrugs her shoulders.

"Yes or no?" he asks.

"All right." He throws the skin into his plastic bag, presenting her with the peeled fruit.

"Tomorrow I'll buy a gift for your baby. I'll go choose something nice."

"Monsieur Sicourelle has already given me five hundred francs."

"Money is money and a gift is a gift. They're not the same thing." She wipes the mango juice from her mouth with her arm. He laughs. He is standing facing her, legs apart. The smell of fried garlic and onion is strong.

She gets up and extends her hand. "Good night, Julien." He does not touch the hand. He moves aside, letting her pass.

2.

Jean-Luc reads all the time, and I'm jealous of his education. I wish I were that educated, but there's no chance. I'm too impatient, I tire of everything too quickly: of reading, of writing, even of thinking about myself — but especially of writing. After I'd sworn I would write every day, a week went by without my writing a thing. On the days I don't write I leave blank pages with a date so that I'll have to confront my laziness.

I don't know why, but I told Jean-Luc what went on between Julien and me. I exaggerated a little, saying that Julien had touched my breasts. I watched Jean-Luc to see how he would react, whether his face would change. It was strange: I almost felt as if I wanted to hurt Jean-Luc, the way you do someone you care about. He started to ask all kinds of questions and suddenly I lost interest. "It's none of your business," I said. He seemed disappointed. "Okay," he said, "if you say so." He took his car keys and left the house and I haven't talked to him since. I've sworn that if I do talk to him again, I won't expose myself in such an embarrassing way. Sometimes I think that talking is far more clumsy than actually doing, worse even than if I was to go ahead and sleep with Jean-Luc.

Anyway, I had just finished my peach nectar when I spotted Monsieur Sendrice, the Cypriot merchant whose house we had dinner at several nights ago. He's insufferable. He sat down at my table and wouldn't shut up — spitting, coughing, lighting half-smoked cigars, laughing like an old lech, telling bad jokes, all the time poking me a little with his elbow. Still, I was happy to see him; for some reason, I like him. He makes great stuffed vegetables. He stuffs everything — tomatoes, onions, potatoes, carrots — all by himself, without a cook. He began interrogating me. "So, what do you think of Erouan?" He was obviously dying to know whether a wedding would come out of this. I played innocent. "I love my cousin very much," I said. The word "cousin" confused him a little. "Yes," he admitted, "he really is your cousin." Then suddenly he had a brainstorm: "But he's not a blood cousin!" "That's not important," I said. "We're just like brother and sister, Erouan and I." We said nothing for a few minutes, then he offered me a ride home.

3.

Eve is hanging off the niece's neck. "Tell her to give it to me, Esther."

"Give you what?"

"My crocodile. She's always taking it from me."

"Give her the crocodile, Priska."

Priska is hiding around the side of the house, panting. "It's not hers!" she calls.

The girls have been left with Esther since the morning. "You don't mind keeping an eye on them for an hour or two, do you Esther?" Madame de Karini asked. "Their nanny is ill and I don't know what else to do with them."

"Esther would be happy to look after them," Madame Sicourelle interceded. "She hasn't got anything to do this morning anyway."

"I wanted to go to the American Cultural Center," said the niece.

"On a Sunday?" Madame asked. "But everything is closed, child. Besides, Jean-Luc said he would come over to take a swim."

Now Jean-Luc is stuffing his feet into his rubber thongs. "I'm off. Good luck."

The niece sullenly watches his slim back as he walks toward the house.

"Want to make chocolate balls?" she asks Eve, brightening.

The girls dry off and follow Esther into the kitchen, leaving wet footprints behind them. "Julien, are there any old cookies around?" the niece asks.

Perched on a ladder, Julien is wiping the pane of a large window. He finishes a wide circular sweep, then folds the rag carefully and descends the ladder. Without a word he produces a large bowl, *petits-beurre*, chopped nuts, butter, chocolate and liqueur. "Anything else, Mademoiselle?" he asks.

"That's all. Thank you, Julien."

He holds out a long strip of paper. "Monsieur Jean-Luc asked me to give you this."

Esther unfolds the paper and reads: "I'm sorry I left so quickly. I'll call you later. Jean-Luc."

"Throw it away, Julien. It's nothing."

Julien crumples the paper, watching Esther and the girls as they throw the ingredients into the bowl. "My advice would be to stay away from him, Mademoiselle."

"What?" she says, startled. "Stay away from whom?"

"From Monsieur Jean-Luc. Stay away from him."

Her face reddens. "What's it got to do with you, Julien? Who asked for your opinion?"

"Who asked you! Who asked you!" Eve and Priska mimic her, giggling.

"Do as you wish, Mademoiselle, but I must tell you what I think."

Eve sticks a finger into the brown mess, then puts it in her mouth. "Stop that!" the niece says angrily. "Don't lick your finger and then put it back in the bowl!"

"She's a pig," Priska says. "We've given up on her."

They form round balls of unequal size and shape and place them on a tray. "Now we need coconut," says the niece. "Is there any coconut, Julien?"

He is hanging onto the kitchen window, scraping the frame with a knife. "No. You can use chocolate shavings and nuts, Mademoiselle; that is what we always use."

"Well, we'll use that then," the niece says, suddenly wishing she could escape. "Come, wash your hands, girls."

She makes a large tent of sheets and blankets for them in the living room. "Go play in there and don't dare come out," she orders them.

"Why can't we come out, Esther?" Eve asks.

"Why? Because this is the jungle. Whoever comes out gets devoured instantly. Cannibals will make her into soup!"

They play in the tent for half an hour, glancing out warily. The niece lies on the sofa, her feet on a pile of pillows. She stares at the television, smoking.

4.

Visited Julien's house on Tuesday evening. Jean-Luc drove me there and on the way he made fun of the giant panda I'd bought for Julien's baby. It was the biggest one I could find. "You could do all kinds of things with a bear that size," he said with a stupid, ugly smirk on his face. I wasn't in the mood for his jokes and I told him so. He puffed out his cheeks and got all red in the face and said as if he were terribly sorry, "Off with his head! Off with his head!" It made me laugh. He can be really sweet sometimes. We've been seeing each other almost every day, and practically everyone is unhappy about it — the uncle, Madame Sicourelle, Erouan, Monsieur Sendrice. Even Julien. After we said good-bye the other day it occurred to me that it's really just the disapproval that creates that spark between Jean-Luc and me. Maybe if we weren't both stuck here like this we wouldn't even notice each other. Jean-Luc said he thinks there's something rebellious about us both. Bullshit. Whenever he sees the uncle he sucks up to him right and left as though he were hoping for a job or something. It's just as well he doesn't know what the uncle really thinks of him. Then again, maybe he does.

Meanwhile, I hadn't noticed that we'd come to one of those black shantytowns. We had to drive slowly because the alleys were so narrow and sandy. Everyone was staring at us, practically devouring us with their eyes. They were all sitting on the ground outside their tin shacks, men, women and children, lighting fires and grilling fish and *manyuk,* that thing that's like leek.

The smell of fish, smoke and sweat was awful, and Jean-Luc closed the car windows and turned on the air conditioning. I was a little afraid. I didn't like the way the people stared at us and I tried not to stare back. I started changing stations on the radio. Jean-Luc asked if I was okay — he knew I was scared. I told him I was fine, I was sure there was nothing to be afraid of. He admitted he'd been scared the first time. Not of something specific, like a knife in his back — it was just a vague sense of anxiety, of distress, as if what he was seeing — the poverty and the filth — would stick to him forever. I felt a little like that too. I was amazed he knew how to navigate the alleys and find Julien's shack without asking directions. I asked him how he knew the way, whether he'd ever visited Julien's place before. Once, he said.

JEAN-LUC STOPPED THE CAR several feet from Julien's house and walked me to the door. He said he'd wait in the car. The door to the house was ajar, but I knocked anyway. No one came. I knocked several more times and wondered whether or not to go in. In the end I did. The room was almost completely dark, although the floor was lit by some light that came in through the broken blinds. I saw a body lying on a mattress, someone sleeping. I thought of just leaving the bear there and going, but something made me stay. "Julien," I whispered. I was sure it was him lying there.

I heard the sound of heavy breathing. "It's me, Esther," I said. Julien sat up with a start and asked me what I was doing there. I told him that I'd come to bring something for the baby. He asked me which baby. "Your baby," I said, "the one that was born two weeks ago."

He opened the blinds, leaned out the window and asked me how I got there. I told him that Jean-Luc had driven me and was waiting outside in the car. Julien stank of beer. He dragged a chair over and told me to sit. "So where's the baby and the baby's mother?" I asked.

He told me they were at the neighbors' and offered me something to drink. I refused politely. He sat opposite me, his legs crossed on the mattress. His skin shone like velvet in the darkness. He was half naked. We said nothing for several minutes. It was so stifling I could hardly breathe. "I will bring you something to drink, Mademoiselle," Julien said finally. He vanished into a dark hole — the kitchen, I guess. Suddenly there was a strange cry. "What's that? What's that?" he said. He'd stumbled onto the bear I'd left on the floor. I jumped up from the chair, picking up the bear and placing it in his hands so he could feel it. "It's a toy, see?" I said. He touched it with his fingertips, as if he were still a little scared, then laughed at himself. "What a fright I had! I thought it was a real animal," he said. We were standing close. His chest was soaked, maybe from sweat, maybe from water that he'd thrown on himself in the kitchen. I've seen him do that, stick his head under the faucet, then shake the water out of his hair. I felt very tense but I liked the feeling. I wanted it to go on, for Julien and me to stand there always. I knew that if I touched him, even with just a finger, the tension would disappear. I said something stupid — "You're completely wet" or something like that. I stared right into his face, something I had never dared do. His eyes were black and his pupils dilated; they looked full of hatred. I'll never forget those eyes and their dark, blank, hateful stare. No one has ever looked at me like that before. I couldn't understand what I'd done to deserve his contempt. For a second I thought that Julien was simply crazy. He was crazy, and I was crazy for going there. Then he said abruptly, "Monsieur Jean-Luc should not be kept waiting too long." I took a step back, toward the door. "You're kicking me out, aren't you?" I asked. He said nothing, just kept standing in the kitchen like a pole, his head grazing the ceiling. I ran out to the car, shaking.

JEAN-LUC WAS CONCERNED. He asked me if something had happened, but I didn't want to talk to him about Julien. I got in the car and we drove off. I leaned back and covered my eyes while Jean-Luc took a small bottle of cognac out of the glove compartment and offered it to me. I drank some and my head cleared a little. I still didn't understand why I was so shaken by Julien, but the familiar streets of the city calmed me. Jean-Luc suggested we stop and have a drink at the Meridian. He talked about all sorts of things and I was grateful that he didn't shower me with questions. We sat in the tropical garden at the Meridian drinking cocktails until it got late. When we stood up to leave, we were both a little drunk.

Jean-Luc asked if I was feeling better when we reached the house. I'd looked quite upset before, he said. I was lightheaded and wanted to drive around some more, but Jean-Luc wouldn't. He said I was completely drunk and needed to go to bed. I tried to argue but I didn't really care one way or another. I felt totally numb and happy. Before I went into the house we sat in the car for a while and talked about what we'd like to be doing in a few years. Jean-Luc said he wanted to be doing exactly the same things as he was now but maybe in another place, Asia or America. Without thinking, I said I'd like to be a diplomat. That amused him no end. "A diplomat," he kept saying, practically choking with laughter. I was lying, of course, but was insulted anyway. "What's so funny about that?" I said. Jean-Luc wasn't listening — he was sputtering and coughing and writhing in his seat. "The child wants to be a diplomat! You mean a diplomatic incident!" I was suddenly sick of him. I got out of the car without saying goodbye and slammed the door. All the way up to the house I could hear his rude drunken laughter. Disgusting.

I took my shoes off at the entrance so I wouldn't wake anyone, but when I reached the door to my room, feeling the walls and the furniture to find my way, I heard the uncle calling me. "*Ta'ali hena, ya*, Esther," he called. "Come here." He had been sitting on the sofa the whole time, waiting, watching me grope the armchairs.

He asked where I had been. I told him the truth, that I'd gone to visit Julien, that he'd had a baby.

I stayed where I was, away from the uncle, facing the door with my back to him.

"Who took you there?" he wanted to know. I told him.

The uncle mumbled something and I could hear the sound of cellophane crumpling and then of a match being lit. "So, he's teaching you about Africa, is he? *El-mouhandes*, the engineer!"

I couldn't answer. I leaned my forehead against the door, hoping he would go away. After a few moments he told me to go to sleep. "We'll talk about this in the morning," he said. I heard him drag his slippered feet into his bedroom.

I was exhausted and drunk but couldn't fall asleep. Every time I closed my eyes I saw the tin-shack alleys, the fires, Julien's outline in his stinking, stifling room. What had I wanted from Julien, and what had he wanted from me? What had I done or said wrong? I felt a cold, wretched despair but no tears. I tried to cry, to force myself to think really sad thoughts about being trapped here, a prisoner, watching my life waste away before my eyes, not knowing when or how I would ever get home. I was alone in the world, no one would stand up for me — not Mother, not Father, not Marcelle, not even Nona Fortuna. Alone as a stone. I pictured myself dead, laid out on a bed of flowers in a white silk dress, my hair to my waist, in my hands a bunch of hyacinths, lovely and white as the walls. Everyone passing before me weeping: Mother and Marcelle holding hands, propping each other up; Father even;

Uncle Sicourelle, wild with grief and guilt. My high school teacher, Rachel, making a speech. "Like a rose among thorns, so was Esther among the maidens." That's what she actually wrote in my autograph book. She asked me not to show anyone: "Like a rose among thorns, so are you among the maidens." I wonder what the other girls would have thought of being called thorns. I would have called a few of them thistles, not thorns. In the end I managed to whimper a little, but only when I remembered how humiliated I had been when Katzowitz, the math teacher, had ordered me to stand inside the wastebasket for an entire class as punishment for throwing some paper out the window.

I dozed off around four in the morning: I saw the glowing hands of the large clock before I fell asleep. As I was finally drifting off, I remember wondering whether Jean-Luc was lying awake, too, like me.

I OPENED MY EYES AT 10:30 with a pounding headache. I lay in bed for half an hour, watching the branches move behind the curtains until I had the sensation that someone was looking at me. The uncle was standing in the doorway, dressed and shaved. He asked if I was awake and I said yes but that I didn't feel too well and thought I'd just lie there a little longer.

He sat on the edge of the bed, covering my legs with the blanket. He reminded me that my birthday was in two days. I didn't really have the strength to answer. He asked me how I wanted them to celebrate and I told him we didn't have to celebrate. But he insisted that we had to. And what kind of fabulous present did I want?

I was overcome with rage; it seemed like part of the pain shattering my head. "Don't try to buy me, *mon oncle*, it won't help," I said, startled at myself. "I am not for sale!" I closed my eyes, curled up under the blanket and covered my face to my nose. I didn't hear him move. "I want to go. Let me go home," I said.

"Why?" he asked. "What's waiting for you there that you want to go so badly?"

"Everything is waiting for me there," I said. "My home is there."

"You're at home here," he said. "This is your home too."

Augustin turned on the vacuum cleaner in the next room and I didn't hear the uncle leave over the noise. Fifteen minutes later Madame came in to see whether I had gotten up yet. She asked whether I wanted to go shopping with her. I told her no. What would I do all day? she wanted to know. Did I have plans?

I had no plans, I just wanted them to leave me alone. I stayed in the house for two days. I can't remember what I did exactly: clean out the leaves in the pool, eat meals, read newspapers, clean out more leaves. I would sit down with a book until I realized I was reading the same page over and over. Jean-Luc called. "You're on African time," he said when I told him what I was doing. I didn't want to see him, and I ignored Julien, looking right through him as if he were air, just like Madame does.

5.

"What's the matter? Are you bored, Monsieur Jean-Luc?" I suddenly heard the uncle say from the edge of the pool, where he was watching. He was wearing a bathing suit. I had never seen him in a bathing suit or in any other clothes that revealed his body. I was astonished. His face and neck were tanned and dark to the chest and so were his arms, up to the line of his shirt sleeves. The rest of him was totally white — especially his huge belly above the black bathing suit. He had taken off the bandage and his wound was exposed. "You should bandage your wound," I said. "The doctor said you should leave it covered for a few days."

"Are you concerned about me, *ya* Esther?" he asked.

"Somebody has to take care of you, Monsieur Sicourelle, if you don't take care of yourself," Jean-Luc joked, getting out of the water and drying off.

The uncle joined him, pouring himself a whiskey. "It's nice of you to find time to think about me, what with all of your affairs, Jean-Luc," the uncle said.

I shrank at his mockery. I prayed he would leave and not make a scene.

"I don't have so many affairs, Monsieur. Work in an office has its routine, you know."

"Of course, of course," the uncle said, pretending to be jovial

I saw he was watching me as I swam. He wanted to know if it wasn't a little chilly to be in the pool.

"It's thirty-seven degrees in the shade today," Jean-Luc told him.

The uncle took a deep breath. "I've been hearing things about your project," he said to Jean-Luc. "Things aren't going so well, I hear."

Jean-Luc seemed to blush. He said there were some problems but he thought things would straighten out. They were working on it.

"Yes, I'm sure you are," the uncle said. "It's important to remain optimistic. So what if it costs another billion? What difference does it make? The main thing is that the machine keeps going."

Jean-Luc sat frozen, not moving a muscle. "I think, Monsieur, that you've decided to insult me today," he finally said.

"Insult you? Why should I want to insult a guest in my house? I look at you, young man, and see only good intentions. Only good intentions."

"What are you saying? I think you should explain yourself, sir," Jean-Luc said, putting on his shirt.

I got out of the water. The uncle quickly held out a towel for me. I asked what was going on, what they were arguing about.

"We are not arguing, *ya* Esther. What have we to argue about? Sit here, dry yourself," the uncle said, lighting one of his stinking cigars. Suddenly I was shivering with cold.

Jean-Luc began to speak very quietly, obviously forcing himself to control his anger. "The fact that we're having problems with the project doesn't mean the whole business has gone bust, Monsieur. There are problems, and we will overcome them. We made some mistakes with the planning. We thought the bridge would hold up at that site. It doesn't mean that all is lost. Mistakes happen — it's only human. Surely you know this, Monsieur."

I didn't understand. "What happened to your bridge?" I asked Jean-Luc.

"Nothing so terrible," the uncle answered for him. "A few million down the drain, followed by a few million more. And all because mistakes are human. You see, *ya* Esther, they can't build a bridge in north Cameroon, where they wanted to. It's impossible to put a bridge there — the topography doesn't allow it. Any five-year-old could have told you that. But the big experts, they like to play games, sitting in their air-conditioned offices in Douala and Yaoundé. They thought they could build a bridge. And why not? They were paid good money to think that way. After all, this isn't France or America, where you go to jail for issuing fake permits. This is only Africa, the backside of the world. Isn't that right, Monsieur Jean-Luc?"

"Is it true?" I asked Jean-Luc. "Did you know that the bridge wouldn't hold up? Did you just keep quiet?"

He started playing with the ice cubes in his glass. "What could I have done? I'm just an insignificant cog, Esther. No one would have listened to me. From the start I thought we should have checked out the terrain more carefully. But they kept reassuring me that everything was all right. What was I supposed to do?"

"You could have resigned," I said to him. "You could have slammed the door in their faces. You could have quit."

Jean-Luc smiled sadly. "You're very young, Esther. Things don't work that way."

I felt disgusted — with him, with the uncle, with all of rotten Africa, with everything.

"At least tell me you filled your pockets," I said to Jean-Luc. "Why are you trying to make it look better than it is?"

"I did all right," he said, taking his keys and leaving.

WE SAT THERE BY THE POOL for about another hour after he left. The uncle kept feeling his shoulder, as if it hurt. "Does it hurt?" I asked.

"It's nothing," he said. "It's much better today." Suddenly he took something out of the pocket of his robe. "Here, you keep it."

It was my passport. Inside I found a plane ticket and some bills — I didn't count how many.

I began to cry. "I don't want to leave you like this."

"Like what, *ya* Esther?" He asked. "What are you talking about?"

"Like this," I said. "In this situation."

"There is no situation. It's all in your head. Life is a situation — there's nothing special about this."

"So do you want me to go?" I asked him.

"I want you to do whatever you want. Go conquer the world, *ya* Esther. You show them."

I didn't understand. Show whom? "Why are you letting me go now, when you wouldn't before?"

"Before was before and now is now," the uncle said, getting up and starting toward the house, dragging his feet. "Before was before and now is now."

I felt not a shred of happiness, not one. I didn't really want to leave, but I didn't want to stay, either. I felt a pain in my chest and a weakness in my legs, pins and needles, as if they had fallen asleep. I opened the passport: there was a note pinned to the bills. I could barely decipher the handwriting. The note said that the money was meant to cover my first few months of studying in France and that the rest should be put in the bank. There was a huge amount of money there, several thousand francs. I began to count but kept losing track and having to start over. Meanwhile, it got dark.

Madame came to call me to dinner and found me with the money on my knees.

"Are you still out here?" she asked, looking at the bills.

She sank into the chair beside me, staring at the water. "You did it, Esther. *Mille compliments, ma fille* — you won."

"What do you mean?" I asked.

"Don't play innocent with me now, Esther, after I've watched you for months, wrapping him around your little finger."

I wanted to throw something at her. "Do you think he should have given it to you? Would that have been better? At least I'll do something with the money!" I screamed.

"You really have some nerve, Esther, do you know that?" she said.

I don't know what got into me, but I stood up and threw the bills in the pool. "Go ahead, Madame, jump in," I said to her.

She couldn't believe her eyes. "Have you lost your mind? Have you gone completely mad like the rest of your family?"

I walked away. From my window I could see her bending over the pool, trying to fish out the bills. Madame doesn't know how to swim.

I stayed in my room the entire evening, starting to get my things together.

The uncle must have gone to sleep. I heard nothing from the

living room. From time to time I peeked out at the pool. Some bills were still floating there, among the yellow leaves.

I wanted to tell Jean-Luc what had happened, to laugh with him about it. All of a sudden I missed him. I remembered how his face looked as he was leaving and the way he kept toying with his watchband with those lovely long fingers of his. I forgot why I'd been so angry with him. Suddenly I felt ridiculous and pompous, pouncing on him like I did. I got dressed and went out to the street, looking for a cab. Augustin had fallen asleep on the table in his shack. He didn't notice me leaving.

THE DRIVER DROVE AROUND for at least twenty minutes, through parts of Douala I'd never seen, neighborhoods full of high-rises. I was sure he was trying to cheat me, but then he stopped in front of one of the apartment buildings. I checked the names on the mailboxes. I had never been to Jean-Luc's apartment although he had invited me over several times to see his photographs. He lived on the eighth floor. I rang three or four times but nobody answered. I was about to give up and leave when the door opened. Jean-Luc stood there in a robe, his hair all messy, as if he'd just gotten up. I apologized for waking him.

I hadn't, he said, peering behind me into the hallway. He looked a bit confused but invited me in. I sat down on a white leather couch. He lit the side lamp and sat opposite me.

"So?" he asked.

"Nothing," I said, looking around the room. "It's clean here."

"That's because it's cleaned," he said impatiently, picking a crumb up off the carpet.

I heard water flush in the bathroom. "Is someone here?" I asked.

"Not really," he stammered but I could make out a tall figure standing in the corridor in his underwear. Jean-Luc looked at me and then at the figure. "Come, Julien, come sit with us," he said quietly. Julien sat down in a far chair, crossing his legs.

Suddenly I burst out laughing and couldn't stop. I was practically in pain. Every time I tried to stop and say I was sorry, I started up again, giggling, hiccupping, even stamping my feet, which I couldn't seem to control. Part of me was thinking that something was wrong with me and wondering what it was. Through my tears of laughter I saw Julien's face become hard, severe. Once or twice he moved toward me, but Jean-Luc said, "Leave her. She'll calm down in a minute."

He brought me a glass of juice. "Drink," he said. I drank, but spit everything on the pale carpet. Julien brought a cloth and kneeled by my side to mop up. Jean-Luc and I watched him, down on all fours, half naked, rubbing.

"I think you should go now, Julien," Jean-Luc said.

I was finally almost completely calm, except for an occasional giggle. By the time Julien came back fully clothed, I was quiet. "See you tomorrow, Mademoiselle Esther," Julien said, leaving.

JEAN-LUC AND I SAT WITHOUT SPEAKING for a while. He leaned his head back on one of the pillows. I thought he had fallen asleep.

"I'll go now too," I said.

"How?" he said in a heavy, sleepy voice. "Wait, I'll drive you." But he didn't move, and neither did I.

"I'm going home," I said. "The uncle gave me my passport."

"Good," Jean-Luc said in the same voice. "I wish you every success."

"What about you?" I asked.

"What do you mean?"

"What will you do? I mean with your project and all that."

"The same. Just go on the same." He was quiet a moment.

"You must be wondering what you just saw."

"I think I know."

"What do you know, Esther? What do you know?" he asked gently, looking at me with affection and sadness.

"Well, that you and Julien are — together." I barely got the words out of my mouth.

"We're not 'together.' This is the second or third time he's been here."

"But there were others before him," I said.

"There were others," he said, holding out a cigarette. "Want one?"

We smoked, going out onto the balcony and looking down at the dark city. "You can hardly see where the city ends and the sea begins," I said, just to say something.

"So, you're leaving?" Jean-Luc said, suddenly reaching out and stroking my head. "What stiff hair you have, Esther," he said, taking my hands between his and rubbing, as if to warm them. "Stiff hair and soft hands," he said, resting his warm lips on my hands.

We hugged. Beneath his robe, which had fallen open, I placed my hands on his protruding ribs, on his slim, narrow, boy's waist.

We lay down on one of the couches, chilled by the cool leather, wrapping ourselves in his robe. We lay in an embrace until morning, not moving so as not to fall off. I dozed every so often, waking in tears or in alarm. Every time I opened my eyes Jean-Luc's were wide open, gleaming in the darkness, waiting.

At six he got up and went to the kitchen to prepare breakfast. I heard the water run, the refrigerator door open and shut. I went and stood in the doorway, watching him. He changed the filter in the coffee machine, not letting on that he sensed my presence.

"It's strange what you have to go through before you realize that you love someone," he said with his back to me.

"Who are you talking about?" I asked.

"You know," he said.

Translated from the Hebrew by Marsha Weinstein

Adapted from the novel THE ONE FACING US, *which Metropolitan Books, Henry Holt and Company, is publishing.*

Batlike, Wolflike (a memoir)

Robert Glück

Waiting

It's not Your Benevolent Majesty's short visits that appall me, but the feverish silence and postponement of your absences. During those stale days and nights my body becomes the keepsake of a golden age: roll this deserted continent over in bed. The moon casts shadows for a week; suddenly it's empty. The silences are just as silent as the rings are noisy. I hear — even before Your Majesty's greeting — the echo and hiss of a long-distance connection. Then I know the taste of victory and joy rains down like tickertape on that narrow electrical street.

Even so, the calls are disappointing, inconclusive. Your Majesty's voice becomes bright; you're vaguely responsible, charming the distance away. "What's new and different?" Your tone assumes it's obvious to both of us you can't be with me.

What does that mean beyond the fact you don't mind not touching me intimately?

In Your Majesty's absence I lose track of who you are, in the psychological sense. I'm as tired as Your Majesty of our phone conversations. My worn-out grievances are painful to you but why should they be? — they prove I never have my way. I exist as points of an argument. Justice is on my side but it won't defend me. Before we see each other I think, "This will be the last time, just a few more weeks" — and that's what I tell my friends. "His Majesty is too —"

To wait all day and then wake up at night and wait. To turn the light on, eyes stony and feeble with sleep. To wait even when you are with me for the end of the story, forever disowned, then suddenly here. To get up to piss, climb in bed, switch the light off, say *I love you* into the darkness, moved by these bold words that reduce experience and focus it on one plane like a projected image. But I'm only whispering in the dark at 4 a.m.

On the bus I see two spellbound passengers cruise each other with such exaggerated eye contact I wonder if they already know Your Majesty. Their lips part, their arms grow weak. The bus is a formal public space but they are contorted inside as mulberry or pine. I wonder how excited they are so I breathe with the closest one, quick and shallow, twice the rate of my breath — he's very excited.

Huge calendars of excited stalemate. My weeping eyes are my whole body. I turn on a made-for-TV movie. I don't relax; I make the movements of waiting, an endless five-minute intermission. Grief weakens my neck — gestures of grief are those of illness and fatigue: my head, supported by pillows, rolls its weight onto my arm. Or has Your Majesty revealed how tired I've always been?

How can I explain to my friends this crisis without a subject? How can I separate my defeat from the defeat they live in their own lives? I like these made-for-TV movies, they express postponement in a way that is not naive. My relation to inner life changed forever when I realized I could just take something. Sophia Loren takes revenge on the cocaine industry for her son's defeated life by becoming an undercover agent. She hides her beauty in the open. After a while I turn it off and do the dishes. I like hot tapwater spilling on my hands and the odor of Lemon Joy. Then I find my checkbook and pay the water bill, a stately transaction, then wander over and turn it back on.

My silence is a machine that produces this kind of program, organized like a courtroom drama. Inside me and Sophia Loren the trees along a riverbank lean heavily over the tarnished silver. The narcissism of this prose is more melancholy than its subject matter: neither wants to lose its loss or budge from the mirror, more thrilling for being empty. Maybe I'll masturbate to add a little tension to this program, a small buzz of existence, a measure of release, fatigue, some spilling and closure.

In other words, I bleed into the night and in memory reverse the flow. The question is not how can I die, but how can I rid myself of frantic bitterness — and indifference. Echoes and delays, empty and dry, a system that escapes my understanding as I become it. How can I interpret your canceled flights so that I still feel the joy of reunion when you arrive? How can I interpret your canceled flights with only the language of canceled flights, the delayed arrivals with only the language of delay, so that I feel the joy of reunion and have it as my own?

TASTED

Yes there His Majesty is, sprawled at the back of the waiting area in Newark, someone's smoke drifting across his lack of expression. He pretends not to see me until I offer my hello, then grows hungry, throwing a nimbus around his hair. His hunger doesn't pertain to me except I seem to satisfy it. Lack of recognition is murder. This is simple and hard to grasp as though written on a blackboard. Anyway, there he is in the waiting area....

He's about to say, "How was your flight?" The welling feeling of arrival: with pride I remember the little bottles, the bunched silver and brown wrappers and empty cans on the suspended table — the plastic tumbler, sharp triangle of lime floating below the surface, dark peel and white pulp, a chip of ice moored against it, each bubble dignified by its spot of light and smear of shadow, the drink casting swimming-pool reflections on the plaid fabric of the seat in front. The swizzle stick capped with a White House — as though sheer description can seduce a secret into speech. The swelling tissue rising on the crest to meet him. To destroy an image, show it by example how delicious one's own blood is. With pride I list the inadequacies, the toilet's vile blue water, my laziness and envy, the woman pulling her collar over her jacket lapel, sting of a light wind, distant corporate thrum, checkered landscape, deviations of some river, light appearing in clusters along its banks. In many books (on the subject) the hero suffers a crisis which leads to well-crafted grief — but the crisis is badly posted. Does the hero lack an identity, a dad? Does he need some action to match his intensity, to throw back his head in his mind, to fall backwards? Outside (of the story) society burns lustrous taillights in the tunnel.

It's all violence and doubt, a white haze behind which His Majesty exalts, speechless with joy. The distant buildings are lost, the nearer ones gray ghosts. Up here you see their classical friezes, swags of laurel I guess, then dentil, bracket and cornice, optimism of the empire, then the vernacular water towers, witches' huts on chicken feet.

His Majesty kisses me too quickly. Only let feelings start and with them the joy of his approval. First he sniffs, tastes, draws back to consider (give him a considering expression). NOW let him vanquish me, let him criticize till I unfold downwards like Venetian blinds, let my face reflect from the bottom of a well. I'm incredibly sorry, my eyes and mouth are circumflexes and three whips of horsehair sprout from my chin. We both think I taste bad, and we're both uncomfortable.

He makes blood flow and his lips curl. Small teeth, pointed tongue. Whiff of iodine. A dry electrical static. He clings to me and desire enlarges his eyes and lips. His face opens out, ravished and open. I recognize in His Majesty a lover I want to arouse, take into my arms forever. I don't own my flavor in the same way I own my life. By forever I mean forever.

His Judicious Majesty draws back. He can't pray so he can't say the food is good. When we first met I was not immediately attracted. We were introduced by friends. It was raining. He sat on my Mission chair with his arms crossed and his nose in the air and I wondered actively what it was like to be blond and lanky and withheld. Sentences drifted. He's going to be the withholding one. He's not only young but young for his age. I will be passionate, inventing forms that force love to appear, hesitant and floundering. His Majesty will judge, will control by advance or withdrawal. I will love His Majesty so freely that I become a good deal, he'd be a fool to pass me up, though His Majesty, like any predator, scorns such easy prey. I will have complexity on my side, being the passionate one, the one who loses.

I pick up the man in shorts from the stupid club His Majesty and I went to last night. The man and I mouse around, neither very excited. His Majesty takes my place. I watch from behind the door — first I join in but pleasure belongs to them. The best I can do is climb into the man's mind. He's being fucked by His

Majesty. He can't see His Majesty (his legs are bent in front of his face) but recognizes the justice in that. He thinks, "The highest sex is that cock's pleasure inside me" — and his own orgasm confirms the accuracy of his thought. I see His Majesty with other men; I stumble on His Benevolent Highness necking with a huge blond. I bow my head and my features hang from my skull, my tongue unfurls and my face tolls like a bell.

EDIBLE

One runs squealing over the threshold and down two steps into the living room, a second follows, a third pauses just an instant to slam the door. Involuntarily his hand guards his throat from unseen attack.

Now the wind jolts the foundations of the entire house and the door is about to cave in. Their faces open downwards in terror as though their skulls were already picked clean of musculature. He likes pork, brutal compliment. For the first time the Little Pigs understand what it is to be loved for your flavor.

They race around, their eyes roll back, blue and white, Delft tiles burst from the fireplace, etched glass shatters — wind hauls them to one side, to the other, braided rugs spin like Frisbees. The world grows angrier. The house is derelict, a filthy concrete bunker with a tin roof. The air is full of blood that fills them with insult when it touches their skin. In the midst of this upheaval the pigs appear tasty to each other; they are caught in his appetite, so simple it shatters their complexity. Their relation to inner life is no longer naive, the assumption of competence is lost forever when they realize they should just take a Valium. Wind hurls diaries and calendars around their heads, pages flap, the terrified wings of game birds.

I'm talking about a catastrophe that is a joke.

Non-Relation

All my waiting collapses in a moment of non-relation. When His Majesty finally enters he shapeshifts into surrogates and proxies, hints and allegations, partial elements and deviations, suspensions and anticipations. His Majesty is not only young but young for his age: he thinks intimacy is a scout troop which he leads. Even if I say His Majesty is just the T his number forms on the telephone's face, just thin electricity, just an excuse for waiting, just the perfect gentleman with thick brown hair and close-cropped moustache, just a style queen who knows a few good moves and dances with his eyes closed, just a space cadet his friends call *Moonbeam,* just His Expected Majesty, that doesn't explain how dull and flattened I feel at the first sight of the medals on his chest, his stupid pageantry and dynastic arrogance, his grizzled beard, his exhausting wealth — an abbreviation grown abstract from shapeshifting whose feet don't touch the floor when he sits on an ordinary chair.

Still, His Majesty reserves for himself the greater depth. I say, "Your Majesty should direct a mental hospital because you hear voices, are prone to fits of howling and are slowly transforming into a woman." My voice is weightless. He stares flatly before replying so the exchange expresses his contempt. I'm what's left on the napkin. The contempt is more important than His Majesty. His Majesty is like a capital city that hoards existence.

Strange to be at the lowest point and deprived of the fragment. I am simplified by his hunger, forever understood. Unity is a disease of meaning. I listen to noises that don't change me — the base line of an approaching car, I am waiting, the base line of an approaching car and a quick cough, chimes meaning wind, a voice in the foreground. On the bright screen a child's hands strike piano keys, barechested Polynesians row a Kon Tiki, a stylish woman finds the taste of coffee delicious and marvels to her friend who appears as the camera draws back. This flatness continues past the two puncture holes. I'm no longer naive about thresholds. A vampire can't cross without an invitation. I have no top or bottom. A woman is exasperated when her relatives persist in using the wrong shampoo. I am a container, I am embarrassed by this, and inside my rapture a ghost longs backwards to the theater of his absence. I want to live again as a widow and resume the guilty pleasure of interior life.

Shapeshifting

His Majesty is the basement of old family names, stiff courtesy, the folkloric costume shoppe, the ham actor's tragic expression, organ music and attar, diminishing, diminishing, until His August Majesty is a flea in ceaseless travel over the skin of a dog.

Wisdom and nobility have devolved on His Majesty's legend with the rest of the bric-a-brac. He's an appetite that caught me long ago, a snake who strikes too low for a good defense.

The Dead One suffers the good taste and piano music — it's not how he acts but how I treat him. It's my drama; he is empty, contingent. I go up or down to become afraid. It is ghost etiquette to remain extremely sociable even though unseen. I put him in the basement like junk, or in the attic with the rest of the junk. Ponderous junk, gray granite and a steady rain. Though essence is long gone, pre-modern water still strikes slate roofs and spills into stone gutters that reorganize it downwards and downwards.

Your Majesty dozes, your elegant face supported by your jacket next to the window. Above you the word Napoli unfurls in a ribbon over medieval towns with towers and ships on a river. I'm almost asleep. My legs drop against Your Majesty's legs but I don't want to lose control of my limbs in a crowded compartment. Emptiness wants me to yield, order wants me to stay the same.

The dead are treated like a Third World country. We hold death against them as we hold poverty against the Third World — as proof of its insufficiency, incompetence — so that we can live comfortably. If they were more competent they would be rich, alive.

A glass of water evaporates because of the air's thirst. The glass holds a pale film of the water's grosser parts, minerals and salts I guess. I shake my fingers as though they were wet with anxiety. Like the young I want to rid myself of not knowing what to do and the bigness of the world. If I am aroused by that evaporation am I in agreement with it? I could say I change because dryness suffers thirst for me, for me.

Attraction to His Majesty is attraction to a change of scale. He does suddenly what I do slowly — fall to dust, retreat through time. He is batlike so let him be a bat, wolflike so let him be a wolf. Moved by the smell of my blood he jumps an existence, reaching in his hunger. I'm flesh for a moment because a zombie wants me. This is not shallow breathing, the two on the bus, shallow passengers. Their bodies' tips are formal as primary colors — a certain number, no more. They build outward from them with them structuring the, as they say, human emotions. This is the lesson of my dreams and daydreams: It's impossible to be different without being aroused. It's impossible to be myself without being slightly dead.

I'm talking about the arousal of defeat, of the body's core and the streaming inside its cells. Put another way, my love for His Majesty is not so much narrated as lit from within.

Genre

I have always liked the horror genre, its corny good taste and corny enormity, that's why I fall in love so easily. I've always liked to scare myself by not noticing the dubbed soundtrack until too late. Then I hear the throb that invites and eliminates feelings as though music were memory. My brand of transgression has always been the outmoded, I've always been attracted to ghosts and obsessions, revival architecture, the mirror, arousal so traumatic it shatters every other scale, the antique orgasm, lightning without ground, the orgasm that cracks out of time like a walnut from its broken shell — I return to the ruins, dwell in them.

Only yesterday I met the good of the bad and the bad of the good. His face was a peony of such distinction its petals didn't touch. I always thought my idea of beauty would change but I caught a glimpse of the antique face of a young Ingrid Bergman through the black veil of the difference in our positions. I mean his face was satiation without thought, boneless and dizzying; I mean a version of beauty stepped forward out of time, its own spirit steps forward from my mind to meet it.

Listening

I pour out my story, gaining some foothold or credence, I hope, in the form of His Benevolent Majesty's attention. His irises are disorganized blue geodes. Nothing written or printed exists for His Majesty. Just newscasts and summaries.

His Highness walks along the riverbank and I tag along a step behind, talking all the while. Just gossip and grievance. Who met who, where, what they said. We stroll past crowds of the entirely powerless; they attempt to speak with their eyes as though they could, to get it said before it says them. My words flow on and on. Dragon Burger is gone from the gates of Chinatown — replaced by Mrs. Fields Cookies. Exhilaration turns to melancholy. Cookies take over the world! I exaggerate my outrage to please him. Enormity and good taste walk hand in hand. In the presence of His Majesty I can say nothing whose opposite isn't truer. To have lived is better than to live.

His Eminent Majesty doesn't question or comment; he locks his hands behind his back. I tag along, imitating his slightly knock-kneed shamble. A row of evenly spaced sycamores organizes the levee into a formal public place; the flat wide leaves are known, and the pale distinguished trunks. The river and the levee can be seen. Each tree stands in a circle of its own shade and the distance in between is arid exposition. The river smells like dry grass. A mosquito tags along behind my ear, blurting and subsiding, subsiding and blurting, oddly loud newscasts and summaries, gossip and insult, generating the sensation, or the awareness, that I'm sweating a lot. I would like to cry fat sloppy tears in order to explain my love for His Majesty to my kind-hearted relatives — it would not embarrass them, but His Reticent Majesty would deny me with a raised eyebrow. What he knows destroys what I know. In his face gardeners prune boxwood into columns, cubes and pyramids.

If he questioned me or expressed opinions or even interest I would adapt my report to meet His Majesty's expectations. He wants to receive information in a pure state, impulses along the spine. I say, "On the 22 Fillmore I saw two passengers hold such exaggerated eye contact I was certain they knew each other." I want to be ignorant of my own life, exchange it for a truth that says one job leads to the next, one person to another. His Majesty likes to keep tabs on everyone; he's probably corroborating the story or finding variants, comparing it with the story told by each of the passengers. Belief that His Majesty knows everything equals the belief that everything can be known. I say, "Your Majesty, it was by losing their way that they had a way at all." Intelligence, His Majesty is aware, is uncertain, fragile and complex. Besides gathering the information, evaluating its accuracy, seeing how it fits into the rest of the mosaic, he attracts meaning, that is, attracts a measure of eros, forcing decisions.

HESITATION

Your Ubiquitous Majesty: the four points of the compass set a limit on everywhere. Your Beautiful Majesty: a face combines purity of form with the indistinct. The spasm of pleasure that contorts your face is my revenge. There are more stars than I ever saw, they are a few years younger than myself, more handsome, richer. I interpret their distance as a greater depth which abolishes my own. I was never so free of that daily news. I prefer to think they seem to intend to appear bright to me, extending forward toward me; in fact to be near them I drove a long way on the interstate through Sacramento and into the Sierras as though to some capital city. The more distance between subject and object, the more place for language. Yet they never raise the subject of my relationship with them and when I do they act like I mean to vex them — as though I dragged them through the subject a hundred times. If that were true, why am I still mystified, ignorant of the outcome — of my future in the astrological sense, romance, business trips, mortgages and co-workers?

I would die for you, I would give you my place in line like a mother relinquishing what is mine without conflict. Your

Highness lives in a different city — I sail over the corn in a herring barrel — sting of a light wind, smell of tar. Still, I sense a hesitation on your part. You bend forward and touch me but inside aren't you standing up, turning away? What constitutes a distinction? "Inside" have you abandoned me, "inside" am I dying? Failure is complex, a bureaucracy of emotions. I didn't know the way until it fell out of my fact-finding report. "Inside" Your Majesty smells like camphor; you're so frail I can't see you, and as if to confirm this you fix on distant points — the generic future, an olive tree. Yes, you lose interest in my face and story and the parts that are Bob; don't you focus more and more on three or four generic points of arousal that lead a separate, almost communal life with others of their kind? "Everything wasted," I think, "his high forehead, his blue eyes and smooth skin." If you equal the common good and if it no longer includes me; if you are the word and the word, which I am also, no longer expresses me; if you are the false word, which I am also; if you are the teeming of cells, which are myself and no longer comprise me; if you are negation, something alien I write into the story. Emptiness agrees to travel along with the little story at the same pace. I use some of that nothing to purvey this congested folklore; and then some of it to heat milk with almond extract, turn on the TV, walk my dog, roll over in bed, endure the city heat, the chiming hours at night. Fool, to invite Nothing across the threshold, to agree with emptiness which should always be combatted.

Over my shoulder pastel streamers of orange and lavender rain on Twin Peaks. The water sleeps in the middle of its fall. It's the image of an irrelevant joy, like the reflection in general. I mean Your Majesty can't lose your loss. I wish these cascades were divesting in a fountain in a movie by Kenneth Anger. The sunset is fast but it's alive slowly as I am alive quickly. The clouds dull and darken, suddenly backlit by cold jasper. I'm supposed to derive comfort from that but I am upside down and the suggestion I need consolation frightens me. Am I already so clearly defeated?

Isn't plotless beauty rankling? — the sting of a light wind, scent of honeysuckle, a few stars as the sky subsides. It demands the freedom to have nothing to win or lose. Your Majesty observes, "I don't see me in your future, in the astrological sense." I suppose giving up risk is what religion means by acceptance, the passionate acceptance of defeat — like Chinese poetry, moon, wind, cloud, mountain, the loss of scale that falls out of the blue like an unexpected bill. It's just THE END, predictable and surprising, a metaphor not wandering eternally but circling leisurely at such and such altitude. The deceptive figure eight. V̇

This story includes a few sentences and some of the tone of THE EMPEROR *by Ryszard Kapuscinski, a study of absolute power that charts the rule and downfall of Haile Selassie.*

TEA

Stacey D'Erasmo

MORNING

The teapot whistles.

"Damn," says Lee. "IBM is down." Isabel reaches from the kitchen table to the stove, pours them both more hot water. Frida Kahlo glares out at them from the wall above the sink where she has been thumbtacked, undimmed, for years. NPR murmurs the morning news.

Lee writes some figures in the margin of the newspaper, adding, subtracting. She pushes her tiny yeshiva-boy glasses up on her nose. "This isn't good," she says.

Isabel takes Lee's hand as they drink their tea, crunch toast. She was up half the night, again; she is so tired — in a twilight condition, despite the late summer morning sun. The polish on her toenails, she notices, is chipping. She is wearing the same faintly retro cotton print dress with the tan and green diamonds that she's been wearing all summer. She needs a haircut. There are many things she and Lee need to discuss, many things that she, Isabel, needs to rethink about her life — many things. So many things, in fact, that she got out of bed at 4 a.m. to jot a few of them down in her little notebook so that she would remember exactly the points she wanted to make to Lee, and everyone else. The tea winds down through her, almost refastens her nerves.

"My father asked me yesterday if I want the business, can you believe it?" says Isabel. Maybe that was what kept her up; he sounded uncharacteristically plaintive on the phone. Guilt-tripper.

"And?" says Lee, figuring. "You look tired."

"I am tired. I'm not sleeping again. And, you know — come on."

"Come on what? You're always like that with him."

Isabel resists the urge to say, *Like what?* but doesn't resist the one to say, "Are you seriously asking me why I don't want to run my father's *dry-cleaning* business? Do you want to be a bookie?"

"Bookmaking is illegal," Lee points out evenly. She folds the paper, reaches for a pad and begins making one of her lists. The gold chain on her wrist hangs loosely, confidently. "Are we out of cheese?" From the airshaft there is the sound of a childish shout, a phone ringing.

It occurs to Isabel, chipping the polish off one toenail, that maybe she isn't in love with Lee anymore. That would be sad, of course, but not so unexpected — it's been years, after all. People fall out of love all the time. Sipping her tea, she contemplates Lee. Lee's hair, which she has recently taken to combing straight back off her forehead, stops, prematurely gray, directly below her ears; it does not curl. Her crisp white shirtfront is still untucked. She will tuck it in at the last possible moment before leaving for work so as to cause the least number of wrinkles.

"I'll be glad when this summer's over," says Isabel idly.

Lee doesn't reply, concentrating on her list.

"And why would I want to do that anyway?" says Isabel.

"I'm not having this fight," says Lee. "I have a case to try today."

"What fight?"

"This fight. The one that's really about your issues." She writes *4) batteries* with what seems to Isabel a self-satisfied air. Lee, as usual, is in denial. But where did she put her little notebook?

"You mean my issues about how you think we should leave New York, where we're *happy*, and I should give up my job, go into dry cleaning and move to the suburbs of *Pennsylvania* so you can have a kid? Are those the issues you mean?" Isabel says *Pennsylvania* in the way she might have said *Transylvania*. "And, by the way, were you planning to take the Pennsylvania bar?"

Lee sets down her pen. "I meant the issues about your mother."

"This isn't about my *mother*. Everything is not about my *mother*."

"All right." Lee finishes her list, folds her napkin in her plate, folds her arms, crosses one leg over the other. Now she is entirely folded, like an unhappy bit of origami. "What are you thinking?"

"Nothing." Isabel realizes, horribly, that she is about to cry. But that might be a relief, it might be better, they could both cry, call in sick, go back to bed all day, some sex would be a nice change, and then maybe she would sleep, finally. Lee probably wants to cry, too, though she wouldn't know it. Isabel stares at her crumb-flecked plate, tracing the familiar aqua squiggle with one fingertip. These plates say it all somehow: so necessary as to be almost invisible, the familiar cracks landmarks of their life together — *turn left at the broken aqua squiggle*. This morning, the plate seems almost unbearably poignant to her. She wants to hold it out to Lee, silently.

Lee says, “I have to tell you something.”

Isabel looks up to see that Lee is not crying at all. Instead, she is quietly determined, poised. “What?” says Isabel.

“I have an appointment to see Melanie today.” Lee’s chin is ever so slightly pointy, a trait which makes Isabel believe in phrenology, particularly since it somehow seems to get more pointy when Lee is being more pointed. It is very pointy at the moment.

“Today?” Isabel is shocked.

“I can’t wait anymore,” Lee says. “I have to know — how many times it usually takes, how much it costs, am I too old —”

“You’re not too old,” Isabel reassures her automatically. Lee’s earnestness never fails to move her, even today, when she is probably not in love with her anymore. “But I can’t go today. I’m busy today.”

“Well,” says Lee. “You don’t have to. But maybe your schedule will lighten up.” She grabs the pad again, writes down the doctor’s address, hands the bit of paper to Isabel. “Six o’clock,” she says.

Isabel glances at the scrap of paper. “I know where Melanie’s office is,” she says. “She was my doctor first.”

Lee looks at Isabel for a moment, then gets up and leaves the room, saying, “I’m in court all morning. I’ll call you at lunchtime.”

Isabel, alone at the kitchen table, doesn’t reply. Far away, she hears the front door open and then close, politely lock; Lee is crushingly considerate when angry. NPR mumbles on. So here we are, at last, thinks Isabel. The penultimate scenes will, later, seem so much sadder than the end itself. She drinks her tea, reflecting that at the beginning it seemed that Lee was the woman she had always been expecting, the precise culmination of her personal history. But all these years later she has to admit that she still doesn’t know a very basic fact: what was she to Lee, what is she?

When she asks, Lee usually says "everything," which is as good as saying "nothing." And now that she's not in love with Lee anymore she'll never know, and maybe that's the key: she chose a woman who can get what she wants but can't describe it. Isabel needs it described. She should have insisted on that. She should add that to her notebook, if she could remember where she left it — but she was supposed to leave for the office half an hour ago.

She gets up from the table and goes to the bedroom closet to get her shoes, quickly, and get to work, but the first things she sees are Lee's clothes, all hanging up and undefended: her button-down shirts (many, most of them white), her T-shirts (many, most of them black), her jeans, her good pairs of pants with cuffs, the four exquisite shirts from France, hand-tailored for her, Lee, the bookie's daughter. With her endless supply of trousers and crisp white button-down shirts, Lee's look is so straight-arrow it's almost decadent. She resembles the good brother in a 30s melodrama just inside of whom is lurking a very bad brother indeed. Looking at Lee's clothes is like looking at Lee asleep, including her dreams. Isabel, standing before the open closet, finds herself falling a little bit back in love with Lee, good brother, bad brother, both of them, all of them, all the possible Lees bodying forth as a sober, neat array of black, white and gray outfits, each one a testimony to her desire to live on the right side of the law, to move forward. Lee's father dresses exactly the same way, and refers to Isabel as "your lady friend." It's not terribly far from the truth, Isabel thinks, considering her dresses and shoes, her belts, her impractical coats, her little houndstooth suit with the short skirt. It is one of Lee's inherited charms: to make of her lover a lady friend, mistress of diamonds and cruises and strapless evening gowns. The bookie had all those things once, or so he says, and then lost them through a series of incredible coincidences. Isabel isn't sure if this is true; Lee always says, smiling, half-proud, "It was before my time."

As she looks over her own clothes, they seem beautifully, and oppressively, singular. The dresses sway as she searches through them, all the drapes and folds falling over her arm secretly, in a secret language. They are *her* dresses, unmistakably, each one a small assertion of self, a phrase. Lee likes the ones that billow and slip, the ones that telegraph their capacity to gather. Isabel likes the ones that fall closely and discreetly around her, the ones that gather her and make of her a single column. And then the shoes: heavy, heeled, with a mien somewhere between the sadistic and the orthopedic. Since cutting her hair Jean Seberg-short, Isabel's appetite for this kind of aggressive shoe has increased, as if to balance the new vulnerability of her neck — although showing that much neck is aggressive, too, in its way.

Isabel stares into the closet; she can't do this much longer, she is going to be late. She remembers the lunch date Faith has foisted on her, some filmmaker, and realizes that she is utterly tired of this retro cotton print thing she's been wearing forever. She rattles the hangers, dissatisfied, and then her hand alights on it, precisely the dress she's been wanting without knowing it. She had almost forgotten about it, lost in the general press of their mutual clothes, too many, really, for this medium-sized closet. They should put some in storage. Isabel quickly changes out of the cotton dress into the slender sleeveless silk one of a purple so dark it looks black. It glides on, sheathlike, subtle, clinging without appearing to cling. She bought it for a party, but the party was bad. The purple-black dress has one small white button at the back, at the top, that fastens with an old-fashioned loop of thick black thread. It gives her a pleasant sense of privacy, of masquerade, as if she could slip through that old-fashioned loop and emerge in some other time, some other place. She feels vaguely guilty — but there's nothing particularly deceptive about changing after Lee has gone to work. When Isabel gets home, Lee might say, "You weren't wearing that when you left this morning," and then Isabel can say, "No, I was tired of the other thing." And then they'll drop it. Because they've been together nine years, more or less, and that, everyone agrees, is a marriage, and in a marriage you drop it sometimes. You learn to drop it. Most likely Lee will be in bed anyway, asleep. Isabel will just glide out of the sleeveless silk dress in the dark, alone, and quietly hang it back up on its hanger.

"I LOVE MAX," SAID ANN. "I WANT TO MARRY HIM." Isabel and Ann, who were spending their fourth-grade afternoons living on a farm and near a river and near a sea in the basement of Ann's house, watched *Get Smart* from underneath the ping-pong table.

Max and 99 were trapped in a room that was painted psychedelic colors; the walls were getting closer and closer together. "Max!" said 99. "I think this room is getting smaller!"

"Him?" said Isabel. "I don't think you should marry him."

"Why not?"

Isabel looked at Max, who was pressing against a swirling orange spot with his legs. "I don't know," said Isabel. She had a secret, which made her feel superior. Her family was going to move soon, away from Philadelphia. It was all decided.

Ann, who was spectacularly double-jointed, unwrapped her leg from behind her neck. "You have to know," she said. Ann was a Baptist. She had been reborn last year at Bible camp; since then, she took Jesus with her everywhere, even to the bathroom. Ann was also extremely good with glue, even though she herself seemed to be held together with string. Isabel did not love Ann, but she was fascinated by her.

"I don't trust him," said Isabel. She was wearing her favorite corduroy jumper with the flower-power appliqué on it, but the pink tights she liked most to wear with the jumper were full of ladders and bits of leaves from that day's game of kickball. Isabel was torn between her sadness that the tights were ruined and the desire to pull at one of the intriguing ladders to make the run lengthen.

Ann cracked her neck, studying the little Max figure on the screen. "I see what you mean now," she said. "He has shifty eyes."

"Yes," said Isabel. "That's it." But she had just made that up, just that second. She felt dizzy from her lie.

Max and 99 got out of the room by talking on the shoe phone. "Hey," said Ann. "I know what let's play."

"What?" said Isabel, still dizzy.

"Come in the yard," Ann said. They went upstairs, past Ann's small happy Baptist mother washing dishes, and out the concrete porch steps into the backyard, not even pausing to put on their shoes. The ground was cold, like needles. Isabel stood shivering on the concrete path, but Ann rushed ahead into the damp yard in her stocking feet, looking around excitedly. "There!" she said, as if a ship had suddenly appeared.

They went into the green plastic-sided shed Ann's family called the barn, although it was smaller than a garage. Ann's family seemed somehow to be rural despite living in Philadelphia; they all had an accent and went to the dogtrack on Saturdays, where Ann, aided by God, often won. Ann pulled Isabel inside the shed. The walls were ridged, with shallow wells between each ridge. There were a few bags of mulch piled in the corner, a wheelbarrow, engine parts, an old kiddie pool standing up on its side.

Ann wedged herself into one of the wells. "Get in the one next to me," she said. Isabel squeezed herself into a neighboring well, which felt nice.

"Pressure," said Ann happily. Then she popped out of her

well. "Wait, wait." She dragged a bag of mulch over to right in front of them. "Okay, now," she said, wedging herself back in. "You be 99. Push!"

They pushed with their feet against the bag of mulch.

"I think this room is getting smaller," offered Isabel and Ann screamed, "It is!"

"Oh, Max!" lamented Isabel. The plastic walls made her voice echo strangely, with a kind of peculiar bounce.

Ann pushed harder against the mulch, grimacing. "I'm getting weaker, 99. Help me."

Isabel concentrated. In dreams sometimes, she could not get her eyes open. The light pressed against her eyelids from the outside, full of shapes, and though her eyelids struggled to raise themselves, they would not fully open. She had that same sensation now, wondering what she was supposed to say next. "Oh, Max," she said again. "What do we do?"

"Let's pray for Jesus to help us," said Ann, putting her hands together. "Oh, Jesus, 99 and I are having a terrible time. We cannot get out." She paused, as if listening. "Okay," she said, nodding. "Okay. Uh-huh. We will."

She turned in her well to face Isabel. She held up her hand to Isabel's ear, cupping her fingers. "Here," she said. "Call Jesus on the shoe phone."

"Help, help," said Isabel. She turned in her well to face Ann. "You try." She held her hand around Ann's ear and Ann whispered into her hand.

"Let us out, let us out," said Ann softly, breathing into Isabel's palm. "Let us out."

Isabel, turned in her well toward Ann, had that same dream-feeling of not quite being able to open her eyes. But the shoe phone seemed to be working, because as she looked at Ann she found she could see her much more clearly than she ever had before: the gentle open angle where her nose met her forehead, the punctuating dark fleck in the iris of her right eye, the faint down along the edge of her cheek. Ann's lips were always red, from biting them. Her skin was so white, and her hair was so black. One thin hip jutted out of her well. But was Isabel still 99, or was she Max? And why weren't Max and 99 married? Ann, carried away by the game, was singing "Go Tell It on the Mountain" into Isabel's palm, dampening it. Isabel's shoulders were beginning to ache. She was no longer sure who anyone was in this game anymore. The shed was cold, and the light inside was pale green, a pale and damp echo of green, flashing over the walls. If Ann let go of her hand, they would both go shooting up into the sky.

Ann finished a verse with one prolonged note, and hung up Isabel's hand. Then, biting her lip, she held her hand around Isabel's ear. "Now you say."

THE PHONE RINGS IN ISABEL'S OFFICE at the Van Zandt Foundation for the Arts. She picks it up. She doesn't feel tired anymore. She feels efficient, having left messages on voice mail all over town.

"Darling," says Lee jubilantly. There is courthouse noise in the background, murmurs, laughter, bursts of conversation echoing in the old hallways. "What are you doing?"

"Did you win?" Isabel closes a file and stamps *Denied* on it. "I don't know yet. I think so. What are you doing?" she says again.

"My job."

"Boring," says Lee. "Come have lunch with me. Meet me at home."

Isabel sits back in her chair. "I can't. I have to do a lunch for Faith, I'm already late."

"Cancel it," says Lee, the bad brother. "Cancel it and come away with me, Isabel."

"All the way to 23rd Street?"

"Wherever."

Isabel gazes at the curves of the little bonsai sitting on her desk next to the electric pencil sharpener. It needs bonsai food or something; a tiny leaf tumbles down through the tiny branches. In her slim purple-black dress, in her pleasantly cluttered office, she sees the chaos of their morning as through a telescope: two small objects at a great distance. She says reasonably, "We're fighting. We've been fighting for a while now."

A moment's silence ensues. Then Lee says, "But what if we weren't?"

Isabel rests her forehead on her closed fist. It would be a lie to say she wasn't tempted. "I don't know," she says.

"You never know," says Lee, and silence fills the line again.

Isabel picks up the tiny leaf and wonders from which branch it fell. She looks for the gap.

There is the sound of quarters dropping into the pay phone. "Isabel?"

Isabel plants the tiny leaf upright on the inch of browning ground moss. "I have to go. I can't do this right now. I'm sorry." She hangs up.

AFTERNOON

Isabel and Ann sat at the dining room table at Isabel's house, doing their Roman projects. Isabel's was making a Roman house. She looked at the sheets of cardboard her father had brought home from the dry-cleaning store. They were flimsy. The two precious gray ones would have to be glued together, for the marble floor. The rest were dull red, a dusty, clouded red, like clay. That was history: Romans made their houses out of clay and limestone. Plus, they weren't even houses. They were compounds, with fountains in the center. They had bathhouses and wine-pressing rooms and temples. Isabel's Romans were wealthy and had lots of children. They would all have their own rooms. She planned to make the fountains last, out of shredded Kleenex. On the corner of one of the dull red sheets, she wrote *March 17, 1968* in tiny letters, then cut it out in a little square, to be glued down later.

Ann unrolled a long sheet of white paper. Her project was a mural of Christians being fed to lions. Authoritatively, she picked up her paintbrush, dipped it in red paint and began painting a long, seeping spot, like a red shadow, along the lower edge of her paper.

"Aren't you going to draw it first?" said Isabel.

"No," said Ann. "I know what happens."

Isabel began measuring out the lines where the walls of the compound would go, drawing them with a pencil against her ruler. The pencil marks were silver, nearly invisible, on the gray cardboard. This, thought Isabel, is the floor. This is the floor now.

From the living room, there was the faint smell of cigarette smoke and the sound of the TV. *General Hospital.*

"I just love Jesus," said Ann, and sighed.

"I know," said Isabel. One of her lines seemed to be leaning; she tried to erase it, but it smudged instead. She regarded the smudge for a moment. Maybe there could be a little inside garden there. Romans could have that.

"I'll baptize you later if you want," said Ann, cracking her knuckles.

"I don't know," said Isabel casually. She did not say that getting baptized might cause her to disappear or become a zombie. It would begin as a game, and then it would be terrible.

Ann did not reply, starting on her first lion. His yellow tail curved energetically several times, whiplike. Through the window, Isabel could see her little sister Jeannie and Jeannie's friend Donna, who always had tomato soup in the corners of her mouth, dropping orange seeds in the bushes outside. The March wind blew through their hair as they bent their heads together, teaspoons in hand, planting oranges. From the living room there was the sprightly sound of a commercial.

"I got this line wrong," said Isabel.

"Just keep going," said Ann intently. She bent over her mural, painting abundant fur.

The smoke in the other room freshened. Isabel knew that her mother would be lying on the sofa in her nurse's uniform but with her white shoes off and her white-nyloned feet on the sofa, her arms crossed over her chest, holding herself in. Isabel made a corner. Her mother would be lying on the sofa, strands of dark hair falling across her face. Isabel thought: Marmee, Bertha, Ma, a ghost. But Cassie was her name.

"I'm hungry," said Ann. "Ask your mom if we can have something."

"I don't have to ask," said Isabel. She went into the kitchen and came back with crackers and a slippery plastic pile of American cheese on a plate. Ann unwrapped her cheese a bit at a time, holding the slice by the plastic, taking a bite of cheese, then a bite of cracker, dropping crumbs into her box of paints. Isabel folded her cheese into squares, fit the squares onto circles of cracker, then crunched down quickly, surprising them, the rough and the smooth together. She wondered if that was religious, to eat the way Ann was, keeping things apart. She wondered if that was a way to get to heaven. In fact, Ann was already very pale, like someone who lived in the clouds. She would fit right in with saints.

Jeannie and Donna ran inside. The front door slammed as they clattered up the stairs.

"Shut up, you guys," said Isabel, going to the foot of the stair. "Mom's resting." They continued laughing, hands placed theatrically over their mouths, clattering into Isabel and Jeannie's bedroom.

Ann leaned over, peering into the living room, as Isabel returned to the table. "No, she isn't, Isabel. She's sitting up."

"No," said Isabel. "She's resting."

"I don't think so," said Ann, still peering. "She's watching TV. Look."

"She's *my* mother," said Isabel, not needing to look. "I should know."

Ann, cheese wrapper in hand, looked at Isabel; her eyes, Isabel noticed, had spokes in them, and the spokes were of different colors: green, brown, green, brown. "I have to go home now," Ann said. She dropped her paintbrush in the water jar. The yellow made a streaky swirl and vanished.

"All right," said Isabel.

At the front door, Ann said, "Goodbye, Mrs Gold," and Isabel's mother, leaning her head in her hand, said, "Oh, goodbye, Annie. See you." Ann, holding her mural by two corners, gave Isabel a distinct stare.

"Thanks for the crackers," said Ann, as Isabel opened the door for her. She held the unfinished mural over her head as she walked away, her half a lion undulating above her in the breeze.

Isabel closed the front door and returned to her Roman house, which wasn't anything but silver lines so far. Who were the Romans to her? Who was she to them? They couldn't see her, huge and in the future, reaching in to rearrange their furniture. She loved the Romans and she hated them, too. When she actually read about them in her book, she tended to fall asleep. She frowned at the smudge on the left. If it was going to be a garden, the master bedroom would have to be either extremely small or moved somewhere else. She went into the living room and flopped into a chair.

Her mother, watching *General Hospital*, lit a cigarette. The cigarette made her look busy. Dark lilac circles of fatigue shadowed her eyes. It was because she was heavy, or so she said; her insides were pulling her down. To Isabel, she didn't look that heavy. In fact, her uniform had begun to pucker at the shoulders and to sag at the waist. The two rings she wore — the ornate antique engagement ring, the plain wedding ring — were loose on the hand holding the cigarette.

"I did a line wrong," said Isabel.

"So just turn the paper over," said her mother in her low afternoon voice. In the afternoons she was dreamy and distracted, like someone floating on a lake. The sofa was her afternoon raft. She rested there, surrounded by important items: her pack of Pall Malls, her lighter and ashtray, the small glass of cold tea with the triangular chip in the rim, as if someone had bitten it, her fat book of Green Stamps. She sipped a sip of tea and said, "I'm just going to rest my eyes for a minute." And then, as she always did, she went to sleep. Isabel stood by the sofa and watched her breathe in and out.

When was it, Isabel thought later, much later, long after her mother was dead and she herself had grown up and moved away, and visited Pennsylvania only reluctantly, when was it that she, as a child, began to feel so full of dread? When, in other words, did she know what was going to happen? She knew that the exact answer hardly mattered. She knew that the exact answer was *from the beginning* and *never.* She knew that her question screened a deeper and more troubling question. When could her mother have been saved? *At the beginning. Never.* When her mother finally did it, she locked herself in a supply closet at the hospital where she worked, swallowing a vast amount of pills, as if to say: *This is the size of my hunger.* Isabel found that as she got older she increasingly referred to her mother by her first name, proprietarily in conversation and ritually in her own mind. All those pills: that was the size of Cassie's hunger, in a room alone, in a hospital in Philadelphia, April 1968. Isabel's completed Roman house rose on the dining room table, the doorways slightly wavy from her struggles with her little scissors, the tissue paper fountains bubbling motionlessly in the ancient Roman air. On the day it happened, Isabel leaned down and peered into the rooms from a Roman point of view; her tiny Roman robes billowed out behind her; her tiny sandals echoed on the marble floors. She felt lonely, and perfect. She walked majestically from room to room. Then she picked up the entire Roman house and stuffed it into the trash.

For every day of the eight days of the shiva she wore a black dress with a stiff bow on the back supplied by Nana, white ankle socks, patent leather shoes and her mother's high school ring on its fine gold chain. The dress began to smell, but she wouldn't wash it. She wore the same dress at the unveiling a year later, her wrists extending past the wrists of the dress, the material tight across her shoulder blades and at the elbows. She ripped the sleeves pushing them back as they drove in from their new neighborhood in the suburbs, where dirt was piled up next to the open pits that would be houses. Heavy in her hands was the puzzle her mother had left her — a woman so hungry she couldn't eat, so tired she couldn't sleep, so lonely she couldn't speak, Cassie. Cassie's sense of irony was keen and crude and was saved from being lethal to her children only because her lack of education made her dramatizations somewhat overblown. Toward the end she often seemed like a girl playing a mad scene in a high school play; she wandered around the house with her hair undone. Cassie adored "The Waste Land," which she had memorized in high school: *April is the cruellest month.*

Later, much later, Isabel hated her mother for that. "The Waste Land" was such a high school poem. She developed her own sense of irony, refined but playful; she disdained Eliot. She was not as desperate as Cassie, with her high school education, had been, but secretly, or perhaps not so secretly, she did still really want to know what, and why, and when. It *could* be significant, she quietly insisted to herself, to pinpoint the moment. There was a woman behind the scrim, at the beginning, and never, and always, throwing the oversized shadows. Cassie Gold. Of course it wasn't tea in that glass. Sometimes Isabel thought she really did know the answer after all, she had always known the answer, and her possession of this knowledge caused her to feel both smug and comforted. In the first year after her mother died, she wore her mother's ring under her clothes all the time, even in the shower, even to bed. It left marks on her in the night.

Standing by the sofa, Isabel touched her mother's sleeping body with her gaze, touched it all over, because recently she had not wanted to touch her mother in real life at all. She thought it would probably be dangerous never to touch your mother again, never to lean against her or hug her or kiss her goodbye, so she touched her all over now with her eyes, for good luck.

Isabel's mother stirred. "What? What?" she said.

"Nothing," said Isabel.

ISABEL WAITS FOR HER LUNCH DATE, who is apparently running even later than herself, at Odile's, where punctuality is at best a side dish anyway. The point of dining at Odile's is effecting the most desirable transaction, emotional or professional, with the least possible visible effort to the accompaniment of the slowest possible service. The food is presented wrapped, bound or veiled by transparencies of pastry crust or rice paper, which is to say veiled in such a way that the provocative shapes of raisins, of figs, can still be made out.

Dangling her feet just above the floor and resting her wrists on a striped velvet bolster, Isabel pulls dreamily at one of the two warm, small puffs of bread that have been delivered to her in a silver basket and wonders if she has been stood up. She'll order anyway, on Faith's tab. Just as she is opening the menu, a dark-haired woman rushes up, as if blown into the restaurant.

"Sorry!" she says, as she approaches the table. "Isabel? I'm Thea."

They shake hands, Isabel rising half out of her chair to shake hands with this Thea who already knows her name. Thea sits down, tossing her sunglasses onto the slate tabletop; she is wearing a tight white T-shirt that shows off her muscles, peculiar and fashionable wide-legged pants and the thick, tire-tread sandals worn by movie stars this year. Her heavy black hair flops over wide, strong features that look Eastern European. Short though she is, Thea seems all wayward force and buoyancy, as if tossed up by a nearby wave. She makes Odile's seem like a beach that she herself, Thea, has just discovered and on which, laughing, she is about to plant a flag of her own design.

"Faith seems to have had a conflict —" begins Isabel as they sit down.

"Lots of conflicts, from what I can see," says Thea with a smile. "Must be hell to work for. She called me at the hotel this morning. We had to do twenty minutes on my making her feel better for canceling. She's so sensitive."

"Yes. Well," says Isabel, as they settle in. "I understand you're a filmmaker?"

"I am," says Thea confidently. "That is, I *cause* films to get made, although not from the acting or writing or directing end. I'm not very visually inclined, actually."

"So — you're a producer?"

"A kind of producer. I function as a catalyst for production."

Isabel looks skeptically at Thea, who is avidly studying the menu, a forelock falling over her pierced eyebrow. "Walnuts," says Thea. "I have such a craving for walnuts and — spinach. In those little phyllo things. Oh, here it is." She sets the menu aside and gives Isabel a direct, searching look. "How are you, anyway?" Her eyes are blue, but such a light blue that it's a little bit of a shock to look into them, like coming into the brightness of day after being inside. Her nose is squashy and has a crooked place in it, like a lightning streak.

"I'm fine. You know. Fine," says Isabel, dropping her eyes.

"Ah," says Thea. "I see." She raises the unpierced eyebrow.

The thought flits across Isabel's mind that when she changed dresses this morning her hand was guided by benevolent invisible forces. Embarrassed by the idea, reminding herself that Thea cannot read her mind, she sits up as straight as she can and signals for the waiter, who is resting like a gilded leaf at the bar. He drifts over. They order. "And a bottle of mineral water," says Thea.

"How do you know Faith?"

"MOMA reception. The Ozu retrospective. It was a terrific coincidence that I was out here —"

"And where are you from?" interrupts Isabel, certain that someone this pretentious is obligated to reply "Paris" or "Moscow" or "Tasmania."

Thea turns her shocking-blue gaze on Isabel again. "Los Angeles."

Isabel spies a thread. "Is this about money?"

Now it is Thea's turn to drop her eyes, slightly. It is just possible that she blushes. "Yes. Faith said —"

"Okay, listen, Thea," says Isabel straightforwardly but not unkindly, because she understands at last exactly where they are — Faith is always doing this, promising everyone the moon at receptions, and here's this woman who flew all the way to New York, expecting it — "I should tell you before we start that while Faith may seem — I don't know, casual, for lack of a better word, she's really very cautious and conservative. In all the time I've been working for her, I've known her to invest privately in a movie maybe twice, and both times it wasn't very much. You'd probably have more luck applying for one of our grants, there's still time this season —"

"I completely understand what I'm up against," says Thea. "But I'm committed to exploring all possibilities. You have to, in what I do."

"All right," says Isabel. "As long as we're clear."

"Like I said," says Thea, "I'm clear. I'm extra clear, actually. I'll be up for hours tonight — after you're sound asleep." She turns her light blue eyes on Isabel.

"Well, actually, tonight I have a dinner date and then this benefit thing," says Isabel briskly.

"Popular girl," says Thea.

Their food arrives in all its semi-opaque perfection. They do, Isabel has to admit as she takes a bite, cook very well here. "So," she prompts. "Tell me about your project."

Thea drinks a great quantity of her mineral water, pours herself more. "No matter how many years I'm sober," she says, "I still drink like a drunk." She smiles, laughing at herself. "Cheers," she says, touching her glass to Isabel's.

Isabel, sipping from her touched glass, cannot tell if Thea is being brave, too open, seductive or — most worrisome — all three. She is not quite sure that she can remember how to play this game. She has the distinct sense that Thea is good at it.

"All right," says Thea. "The project. The idea is —" She makes a chaotic gesture with her hands. "I'm nervous. Can you believe it? How long have I been doing this? All right. The idea kind of centers around thirty years in the friendship between a lesbian and a gay man. I've been working with this amazing screenwriter in Santa Monica, a very prominent man, totally closeted until now, but his health concerns — well — anyway, he wants to come out, finally, and the script so far is extraordinary. Oscar material." She pauses to eat several splendidly complex crescents, webbed in nutmeg.

"What else has he done?" says Isabel.

Thea names several well-known movies, one of which is currently displayed in great quantity in the new releases section of the mammoth chain video store in Isabel's neighborhood. Thea names facts and figures, various stars that long to be involved if only they dared, startling demographics, a revolution on the brink, it seems, in celluloid. She is, thinks Isabel, very passionate about this. It surprises her, though she knows it shouldn't, that a person can be an operator and a believer at the same time. The restaurant crowd slowly devolves into a relaxed few as Thea finishes her pitch and crosses her silverware on her plate.

"And so here we are," says Thea. "I can tell you get it."

"I do," says Isabel. She drinks her mineral water, flummoxed, interested. She is so thirsty.

"So should I write this up as a proposal for Faith? Maybe you would read it over for me?"

"No," says Isabel. "It'll end up under her desk. I'll talk to her myself."

"I'd be very grateful," says Thea sincerely, then, with relief, "I'm so glad that part's over." She sighs, pushes her palms through her hair. It flops back down again, *ponylike.* As the waiter clears away their plates, he winks at Isabel.

There is a small silence. Rings of water from their glasses pool on the slate. The afternoon begins to unwind; it occurs to Isabel that maybe she shouldn't even bother going back to the office. It's already past three. "I have a friend who just moved to L.A.," she says. "An actor."

Thea nods seriously.

"I think he lives on a hill or something." Isabel pauses. "I've never been there myself, actually."

"It's a big place," says Thea. "I live in — well, you wouldn't know it. It's this part that's on a canal near the ocean. Very cool."

Isabel ponders what "very cool" might mean to Thea. "It is big," she agrees. "I think he's had a hard time meeting people."

Thea reaches into her jacket, pulls out a pen. "Here," she says. She turns Isabel's wrist over and writes a number on her palm. The pen presses ten times abruptly, lightly, into Isabel's flesh. "Have him call me." Her light blue gaze is utterly clear, nearly transparent, the earnest, slightly absurd gaze of a salesman inviting the customer at the screen door to marvel at a vacuum cleaner. *Why don't I come in and show you how it works?*

"Oh, well," says Isabel, withdrawing her written-on hand. "Thanks." Then she hears herself offering — what is she doing? — "You know, this benefit tonight, it's at The Rack —"

"Oh, sure," Thea says, "I know The Rack." The waiter languorously drops the pumpkin-colored little dessert menu on their table and Thea casually glances over it.

"Right," says Isabel. "Well, there will be lots of theater and film people there, if you don't have something else —" So she is trying out the vacuum cleaner, and the useless attachments. So what? So what if she is? She's an adult.

"Thanks," says Thea. "Maybe I'll stop by. Would you like to split a dessert? I'm a fool for the orange rind baklava."

ISABEL'S FATHER STOOD NERVOUSLY at the head of the table, holding a suit jacket. Unclaimed clothes from the store covered the table and the floor. They did this now and then. Everyone in the family was allowed to pick; the rest went to charity. "Choose what you can use." Isabel had already commandeered a provocatively gold curtain to be cut up for Roman tiles. It lay next to her at the table in a glamorous, exhausted heap. She paused in her search for the other curtain to admire her father's slender pale neck and the chain around it. Even in the summer he was pale from being in the store all the time. As always, his hair was precisely parted, with exact comb marks. His wrists were delicate; he wore a thick gold chain on the right one. My father, thought Isabel, is like a bracelet. No, a bureau, with three strong drawers.

"I've been refining the plan," he said, and cleared his throat. He sat down, jiggling his leg.

In the living room Isabel's mother sat watching *Carol Burnett*, wreathed in smoke. Her face was impassive, the creases deep and intelligent. She absently pulled a checkered scarf back and forth between her fingers. It was the only thing she had wanted.

"Let's move *soon*," said Jeannie. "Let's have dogs." Next to her place at the table was a tangle of pants and a monogrammed ski hat.

"We can't move until school's out," said Isabel.

In his soft voice — he never raised his voice — Isabel's father explained that there was a very expensive, special machine he wanted that could clean your clothes in forty-five minutes: you, the customer, the commuter, in at 7:15 a.m., out by 8 a.m., sipping your coffee and listening to the radio, your freshly cleaned clothes hanging inside your car, encased in long, beautiful sheaths of transparent plastic. Once he had enough money for that machine, which wouldn't be too long now, probably by the summer, they could move. They could leave Philadelphia, where the neighborhood had gone downhill, and live where the neighborhoods were all new, everything in them new, new school, new friends, new families. They could buy a brand new house, instead of living in this old and dark and tilted one, which belonged to Nana, whose feet overflowed her shoes.

"I don't want to go to school anyway," said Jeannie. "I want to work in the store."

"Well," said Isabel's father. "That's very flattering, Jeannie." Jeannie loved machinery: the steamer, the dolly, the ancient washing machine with the mangle in the back. She loved Ari, the presser, who operated the machine that was also called the presser. Anything that the presser put into the presser came out dampish and amazingly flat.

"Are Ari and Louise coming to the new store?" said Isabel, sensing a flaw. Louise was the shirt person. She had hazel eyes with long eyelashes, and was very nervous. Her only son, who also had hazel eyes with long eyelashes, was in Vietnam. His picture hung over Louise's table in the back, watching over the shirt boxes.

Isabel's father waved his hand in a sweeping motion. "There are jobs," he said. "I'm not the only plant in town."

"But Uncle Dave —" said Isabel.

"Of course, he's coming. I've been trying to convince him to move, too. He really should get his own place." Dave worked in the back with Ari and Louise, eating Slim Jims and drinking RC Cola all day. He lived around the corner with Nana in a house where canned soup and tuna fish tumbled magically out of any closet you opened. Although he was already bald, Dave found Nana's closets, and many other things, very amusing. When Isabel's mother met Isabel's father in New Hampshire, it was because he was there with Dave, for the skiing, and Dave was the one who spoke to her first. He told her a joke. Isabel's father didn't know she was a nurse; he thought she was Cleopatra. She didn't know he was a dry cleaner; she thought he was a skier. Isabel always imagined their meeting like that: her mother all made up like Cleopatra, her father trim and neat as a bureau, on skis. That was like a little play itself. "Hello, Cleopatra." "Hello, skier." She went back to Philadelphia with Isabel's father and Dave, and had

Isabel, and that was a generation. Her mother was the first generation. Seen from that perspective, the perspective of generations, it made sense to move. Possibly, Isabel hoped, west. If they moved west, they could live underground, in a sod house with goats running around on the roof. They would have to whitewash the walls every spring.

Isabel's father took a ballpoint pen out of his pocket and got a yellow legal pad off the sideboard. "All right, then," he said softly. "Let's make a list of what we have to do."

"We need three big dogs," said Jeannie. "Their names should be Larry, Curly and Moe."

Isabel said, "That's so stupid, Jeannie," but she said it softly, her attention drawn by the unclaimed suits and ties and dresses and sweaters and blouses on the floor. One blouse was lilac, with ruffles everywhere. It lay on top, the queen. Who had not come to claim it? And why? Isabel felt sorry for the forgotten blouse, tossed into a pile of rude strangers, the suits with voices like old men. Maybe the sweaters were nice, if a little stupid, the thicker ones the stupidest of all. The gold curtain was all Isabel wanted, although she was frustrated not to have found the other half; the rest of the heap seemed dismal and forlorn and haunted, all the unclaimed things on the verge of rising up again, full of people. She felt sorry for them, and afraid of them too.

"Boxes," said Isabel's father. "We should all begin collecting boxes. Sorting our things. And Nana wants us to paint. She's going to use this as a rental."

It was oddly exciting to Isabel that soon other people, other families, would live in their house, people who might find one of her barrettes, a drawing of Jeannie's, and say, *Look, this was who lived here long ago, in history.* The thought made Isabel feel simultaneously ill and happy and strangely powerful, as if she could spy on them, the new people, after they moved in. She could learn everything about them, one of them looking up from her book to say, *What was that? Did you hear that?*

Isabel's father said, "Masking tape. Newspaper."

Jeannie said, "A map."

Isabel smoothed her gold curtain over her knee. Maybe she wouldn't cut it up after all. Maybe she would hang it in her room in the new house. Or it could be a Roman robe. She wrapped it around herself; now she was a Roman and immediately understood the phrase *the sands of time*, because that was like Romans, hiking over the sand in their sandals. Her robe was scratchy, but that was clearly part of the Romanness, so she didn't take it off.

"You know —" Isabel's father tapped the pen on the table. "Maybe we should look into building something entirely new. They're doing that a little farther out, past Darby. I think Dave knows a guy." He wrote down on the list, *Contractor?*

Isabel said, "I want a window seat. Put that on the list."

Jeannie said, "I want a blackboard."

He wrote it down. "Cassie?" he called out brightly, the comb marks all flowing toward her as he lifted his head. "Any requests?"

There was no reply. They waited a moment for her to speak, poised around the table like three people in a diorama. Jeannie put on the ski hat. Isabel's father tapped, tapped his pencil. A laugh crested and fell on the television. Isabel adjusted her Roman robe. Perhaps her mother hadn't heard him. But no one asked her a second time.

AT SIX O'CLOCK, STEPPING OUTSIDE into the late-day heat, Isabel hails a taxi to go the short distance to Claude's, the most wonderful department store in the world, a store which somehow requires that one arrive and leave by taxi. Claude's sits, like the lions guarding the New York Public Library, on a gateway corner of 14th Street; from its antique sandstone side stretches block upon block of cheap department stores, like a parodic reflection, crammed with polyester, knock-offs, three-for-one underwear in plastic packages, bad toys that probably explode when you get them home. Outside of these stores, sidewalk vendors stand by cardboard bins stuffed with socks and T-shirts and sunglasses tinted a weird purple-pink; in the doorways of the stores, plastic rocking horses bobble back and forth, waiting for riders to break them, radio music plays loud, mechanical monkeys hop, and mechanical fish swim on the pavement. In the windows of the wig stores, blond and black and auburn ringlets drape to improbable lengths, like mermaid hair.

The taxi stops. Isabel pays the driver, smiles at the doorman as he holds open the door for her, enters the store and is immediately calmed by what feels like centuries of luxury, some grand ancient city, like Atlantis. Her shoes click on the swirling marble floor. All of Claude's mermaids — the silver bracelets, the cashmere sweaters, the salespeople — rest quietly within, flicking their expensive tails slowly, behind glass. Behind them sit elegant fish-tanks, narrow envelopes in which fish swim among jewelry. Fins carelessly brush along pearls. Climbing the broad, circular staircase, a majestic structure that must be ascended with a quietly majestic air, Isabel hears the music changing on every floor. The Rolling Stones metamorphose into some sort of rainforest chanting as she arrives on the fifth floor. A person could live on the fifth floor of Claude's; in her heart, she does live there, like the children trapped overnight in the Metropolitan Museum in that book. The fifth floor is a ruin that contains bits of everything, a fascinating heap of outerwear, innerwear, housewares and various merchandise from the lower floors that has aged badly and has nowhere else to go.

Everyday life, in the mind of the eponymous deity, is evidently bursting with opportunities to bare your breasts, or at least a significant portion of them, tentatively embraced by buttonless wrapped blouses that open to the waist and sweaters that seem to be made out of angora spider webs. Everyday life, on the fifth floor of Claude's, is something to stalk through, clutching a silk scarf. It seems to include garden parties, exotic dancing and a madcap go at the Iditarod in flame-colored, fur-trimmed Mylar. Suits just barely require pockets, and even then preferably only the implication of pockets, invisibly stitched shut until the rightful owner slips her hand into them, like Cinderella sliding her pale and trembling foot into the glass slipper. Isabel owns one jacket from the fifth floor, a plum-colored orphan, much reduced in price, whose skirt had long since disappeared. It gave her great satisfaction to unstitch the pockets with a small, sharp pair of scissors, cutting the perfectly matched plum-colored thread. She wanted to do it with her teeth, but stopped herself. In this jacket, she knew, she was fabulous.

Today, sleepy, she drifts along as rain patters on a xylophone. She pauses on a rack of pants suits, each one boneless and light in the way of suits these days, the only skeleton yours. Lee would look nice in one of these, as would she, but not worn in tandem: they are alert to the stealthy vocabulary of merging. Anyway, the price tag runs to four figures. Next to that rack is another of teensy neon T-shirts, or half T-shirts, like a rack of angel fish escaped from the tanks downstairs. With her free hand, Isabel holds a chartreuse one up against herself and looks in the mirror. It would fit probably, but what to wear with it? Hot pants? She can't. Maybe to wear to bed? Even the fantasy is hard to pull off.

She moves away from the half-shirts and finds herself in a thicket of dark, wide-legged pants, like the ones Thea was wearing. She checks the tag: a designer, yes, but his secondary line, the one that only bears his initials and is infinitesimally less expensive. But today these pants are half-price. She wonders if this is a sign. Picking a pair in her size off the rack, she ducks into a dressing room, glaringly lit in the manner of all dressing rooms all over the world, a reminder that Claude's is, at heart, just another department store. She takes off her shoes, but not her dress, carefully hiking up the sheath of silk and pulling the pants on under it, zipping them up, buttoning them. They are too long, pooling at her feet, unhemmed. Although skillfully and pleasingly cut for room in the hips and the legs, the material is slightly coarse, one of the new blends that looks better than it feels and dry cleans badly. Isabel's father wrote a letter to the Dry Cleaners Association Newsletter about exactly this deceptive blend, in fact. Is this how the pants feel on Thea? Are they too hot for summer? Doesn't she mind that? Did she buy them half-price somewhere in California and now wear them to meeting after meeting, pitching her movie, sweating a little but trying not to show it? Does she wait for them to be pressed each morning, standing in her hotel room in her underwear, her hair wet, making calls?

Isabel regards herself, wearing Thea's pants. They are flattering, even unhemmed. They looked good on Thea, they look good on Isabel. They would look good on Lee. This spoils it a bit for Isabel, as if Lee has horned in on her private sartorial rendezvous. It occurs to her that she is being a creep. She steps out of the pants, and her dress drops back down over her knees. It nips in slightly, discreetly, at the hem. She puts her shoes back on, undoing and redoing the buckles. Her feet are already tired from walking in these complicated shoes all day. She carefully clips the pants onto their hanger but does not return them to the rack. She hangs them in the dressing room for the saleswoman to find later, like a handkerchief with lipstick on it left in a cab. The traces of a secret life. Then she sits down for a minute in the small overlit room. Parrots call to wooden flutes; leaves rustle. She closes her eyes. There is a swimmy feeling in her head, the familiar vertigo of insomnia. She feels scorched from lack of sleep, but just around the scorched edges, the faintest aureole of a question appears, a thought so unbidden it seems barely to be her own: This Thea, this mysterious and pretentious Thea, woman of the deceptive pants — will she show up tonight?

Evening

Night was falling when Isabel and Ann realized they had somehow missed "Raindrops Keep Falling on My Head" on the countdown and would now have to wait until next Sunday. In despair, they kicked at the shiny floral bedspread on Ann's bed.

"Do you want to go home?" said Ann.

"Not yet," said Isabel.

"Do you want to watch TV?"

"Uh uh," said Isabel. "Let's do pressure."

"It's too late," said Ann. A black curl hung over her forehead in a disappointed way.

"We can go under the ping-pong table," said Isabel. "I have a new idea." They hopped off Ann's bed and went down into the basement.

"Let's take cushions with us," said Ann, pulling the basement sofa apart. Isabel crawled under the ping-pong table and Ann followed, dragging the two long sofa cushions, which were rough, slightly strawlike and dark orange. It was dark under the table. Ann arranged the cushions in a line, then wiggled on top of them, crossing her legs Indian-style.

"Okay," said Ann. "Now what?"

"Lie down," said Isabel.

Ann stretched out and closed her eyes.

"Take your shoes off."

"You do it," said Ann. She was smiling with her eyes closed.

Isabel lifted off Ann's shoes, leaving her socks on. Ann's feet were warm and small; she gently waved them back and forth in their thin, white socks. The underside of the ping-pong table was like a roof, covering them. Upstairs, Ann's mother ran water in the kitchen sink.

"Now —" said Isabel, taking a breath.

"Wait," said Ann. "What's this called?"

Isabel thought for a moment. "This is called — matching. Romans invented it."

"All right." Ann looked pleased to have this information.

Isabel lowered herself slowly, slowly along the length of Ann's body: first her shins, then her knees, then her belly, then her chest. Ann's legs pressed into her legs. Their hip-bones bumped, then Isabel shifted over and they fit. Isabel stretched her arms along Ann's, stretched each finger out to cover each of Ann's fingers. Ann opened her hands out flat, so the pads of their fingers touched at the peaks. Isabel lowered her head next to Ann's, burying her face in Ann's hair. Ann breathed in, then out. She smelled like crayons. Their shoulders, Isabel could feel, were more padded than their hips; their shoulders could rest on top of each other very easily. Beneath their shirts, their flat nipples met. Neither of them spoke. Dishes clinked upstairs. Ann turned her head away from Isabel's head, revealing her neck, her ear. Ann's wrist pulsed against Isabel's.

"Okay," said Ann. "Okay."

"Okay," whispered Isabel. Her entire body felt golden, even the knobs of her knees. "We're moving away," she said. Ann lay perfectly still, moving not one muscle, and said nothing.

They lay like that for two minutes more, and then they got up and together put the cushions back on the sofa. Ann walked Isabel upstairs and to the door, stood there silently while Isabel put on her coat, her scarf, her boots. Isabel thought with pleasure of her Roman house and its dusty red walls now standing, almost finished, on the dining room table; of the new house they would soon have outside of Philadelphia, their incredible, possibly all-electronic house of the future.

Ann leaned against the doorway, one foot up on the other knee of her red hip-huggers. "Goodbye," she said, biting her lip.

"Goodbye," said Isabel blithely. She turned away into the cold. She ran her hand along the black rail next to Ann's three front steps. It was cold, too, like a black tube of ice.

On the last Saturday in March, Isabel and her mother found a house. They drove far past Philadelphia, into the country, the newspaper with the circled ad between them on the seat, the radio playing. On the news, the talk was of Vietnam.

"Will Dad have to go in the Army?" asked Isabel.

"No," said her mother. "He has a family." A wide headband held her hair back, and she had pushed her sleeves up as she drove. She sipped from a mug of tea she had brought with them in the car. She seemed to be in a good mood, as the countryside spun by. "This is like where I grew up," she said. "Look for cows, Isabel."

Isabel counted several cows, not a single one walking anywhere. They turned down a road, then another, passed a little store, then rumbled onto a road that led to the top of a hill, where the house was. The agent's name was Madge, and she met them at the peeling front door. Everything about Madge was wrinkled except her feet, which were beautiful in white slingbacks. She led them around, pointing things out in her raspy voice. She was skinny as a piece of celery.

The house wasn't particularly nice, in Isabel's opinion. There was an enormous water stain cascading down the living room wall, and the kitchen wallpaper was peeling. Pairs of boots of different sizes sat up on a muddy shelf in the kitchen, close to the floor. The living room was full of books stacked up like firewood, none on shelves. There was an intriguing small door cut into the side of the staircase. Isabel rattled the handle, but it wouldn't open.

Madge sent them up the steep wooden stairs alone. "You break it, you buy it!" she rasped out, then laughed a deep laugh, as if that was a very hilarious joke indeed. Isabel wanted to tell Madge how stupid that was, that they weren't going to break anything, but didn't, following her mother up the stairs. Despising Madge, she resolved to be super polite to her.

"Oh, look at this," her mother said, when they reached a narrow room with a painted floor and a small desk set all by itself in the middle of the floor, like an island. Against one wall was a mattress on the floor, covered by a chenille bedspread. From the desk, out the odd, oblong window, Isabel could see a field. In the field there was a car up on cinderblocks. All its doors were gone. There wasn't anything else in the room but the bed, the desk, the desk chair and the window with the field and the car in it. Beyond the car, the land sloped and fell away into woods. Isabel, squinting, took a picture of it with her mind so she could think about it later.

Isabel's mother lifted the lid of the little desk. Inside there were maps, some thread, a yo-yo. A book about the birds of South America. "They must travel," said Isabel's mother softly, dropping the lid back down.

They went downstairs. Madge walked them through the backyard, proudly pointing out the rosebushes, which were little more than a few stringy bundles of thorns. "How lovely," said Isabel loudly to Madge.

They walked past the car, Madge, in her slingbacks, giving it a wide berth. "They'll take that with them," she said. Isabel peered at the car, wondering if there was anything interesting left in the glove compartment. She attempted to excavate it with X-ray vision, but nothing happened. These people, she thought, were poor, and not nearly as smart as the Romans, who built aqueducts.

The March air tipped all of their noses with red as they walked, bit their cheeks. Isabel's mother put her arm around her, and Isabel held her breath. Then she couldn't help it. She moved closer, hard. "Whoa," said her mother, stumbling. They walked together into the wind, awkwardly, hip to hip. Isabel noticed that her head was not so far from her mother's shoulder when they stood side by side. She would be so much taller than her mother when she grew up. Isabel put her hand in her mother's coat pocket and felt crumpled Kleenex, some change. A quarter, a nickel, she figured out. Two pennies. From the yard, Isabel could see the peaked window of the room that would be hers, because it was clear that this was going to be their house, and they were all going to live there, and paint it over. Isabel's room had eaves. Jeannie's room didn't. From her window, Isabel would look out over the yard and muse on the empty car until she grew up and moved away.

Sitting in the living room, in chairs covered with Indian print bedspreads, Isabel's mother discussed prices and taxes and land with Madge. "This is the one," she said. "I just know it." Isabel noticed a stain on the Indian print bedspread her chair was covered in, and wondered what had made it. The stain was the shape of Texas, more or less. Or was it a shark, upside down? Madge and her mother talked on and on, until the sun began going down. The house grew colder.

"Thank you so very much, Madge," said Isabel, as they finally got into their car, and shut the door on her.

Riding home, they were happy.

Later that evening, a fight ensued. Isabel's father said, "That is not a commuter neighborhood, Cassie. That's rural. They don't need a dry cleaner out there." Isabel's mother picked up her plate, and sat alone in the kitchen, staring at her food, while the three of them silently ate dinner. After a while she put on her coat and walked out the front door into the front yard, in the dark, leaving her food behind. There was a flash as she lit a match. She stood there a long time, the lit end of the cigarette marking where she was, like X marks the spot. Isabel, eating peas one by one, wondered if her mother could live in the backyard, maybe in a tent, with a lantern. They could bring her dinner in a basket. At night, from the house, they would see the lantern light shining through the walls of the tent.

ISABEL CLIMBS THE STAIRS TO THEIR APARTMENT. Summer heat clings to the heights of the staircase, the upper hallways, like fog on a mountain top. She shakes out the old key and stands with it for a moment, running her thumb over the worn surface. It has been a long day. She puts the key in the lock and opens the door. The apartment is dark, except for a light in the bedroom. Lee must be awake. Isabel drops her bag on the table, slips off her shoes. Her feet, trained all day by the beautiful shoes, meet the floor in unusual places.

"I'm here," she says softly, checking the mail in the kitchen light. A bill, a postcard from Andrew in L.A., flyers, junk. "Another fucking day in paradise," he's scrawled. "No work yet. But the light!" Isabel tries to remember where it is, exactly, that he lives; did he ever mention a canal? And how could that be anyway, a city near a river near a sea? It's probably some kind of glorified ditch. She slides her belt out of its loops and drops it on the kitchen table, pours a glass of water from the pitcher in the refrigerator, arching the balls of her tired feet against the linoleum. In the sink, there is a bowl, a fork, a glass: dinner for one.

Isabel walks into the bedroom and finds Lee dozing by the bedside reading light, her book falling from her hand. Something about the Mob; Lee loves those. Gangsters around a kitchen table, cracking walnuts, cracking heads. Isabel folds up the Mob and slides next to Lee, picking up Lee's arm and putting it around her. She rests her head on Lee's chest and pokes her blanketed foot with a bare one.

"Hey," says Lee, waking up a little. "What is it, traveler?" She pats Isabel's bottom, smoothing out the silk. "Were you wearing this when I left this morning?"

"No," says Isabel.

"Kind of funereal."

Reaching behind her, Isabel unbuttons the old-fashioned button, then kneels on the bed and pulls the dress off over her head, dropping it, like a shadow, onto the floor. She lays on top of Lee in her underwear, the cotton blanket and sheet between them, kisses her hard.

"You didn't show up," says Lee, fully awake now, turning her head.

"I know that," says Isabel. She rolls over and sits up again, leans against the headboard, a gaudy thing with cherubs they bought at an auction with Dale and Bob. Ornate grapes, offered by one rosy hand, press into Isabel's spine. The room is messy, cold, quiet. Lee puts on her tiny glasses, picks up her book and begins reading. Several minutes pass; Isabel, leaning against the headboard, grows cold. "You have that air conditioner up too high," says Isabel. "It's almost fall."

"I was hot."

Isabel clambers off the bed in her underwear and hangs up the dress in the closet. She unhooks her bra, takes it off and pulls on the tank top she sleeps in, an oversized white one with armholes that reach almost to her hips. She is simultaneously completely worn out and wide awake, as if she could stay up, or sleep, for days and days and days. She pauses at the foot of the bed to look at Lee, who, though ostensibly lying there peacefully reading about the Mob, calm as toast, is actually waiting, Isabel knows, for Isabel to say something. That is, in fact, why the air conditioner was set to high: Lee wanted to hear it clicked off when Isabel came home, to have her sleep ruffled. In this way, half asleep, she might catch an apology. Isabel hesitates. In her striped pajama top Lee is stern as a priest. Sullen, wounded and prone to sudden eruption.

"So, what did Melanie say?" asks Isabel gently.

"Lots of things." A lumpy gangster face, smoking a cigar, stares out at Isabel from Lee's lap.

"Are you going to tell me?"

"If you want. Tomorrow, maybe."

Isabel dials the air conditioner down and gets back into bed, under the covers this time. She moves over to Lee, who silently accepts her into her arms as she turns a page. A small victory for Isabel, who presses her face into Lee's neck, slides a hand under Lee's pajama top to rest on Lee's warm belly. Anchored there, she is happy. One page turns, another.

Lee puts a hand on Isabel's hair. Another victory. Isabel refrains from remarking on it.

"Lee."

"What."

"I never sleep anymore."

"What do you mean?"

"I'm afraid I'm getting like her."

"Your mom?"

"Yes. Before. In the middle of the night she'd be sitting on the sofa, smoking." Isabel pauses. "I'm so glad I quit smoking."

Lee puts the gangsters down. "It's over," she says. "It's been over, for so long."

"Thirty years," says Isabel.

"That's a lifetime," says Lee, picking up her book again.

"Yes, but how can we — you know, I just feel so fated to pass it all on somehow, even if I'm not the one —"

"You are not fated, Isabel," says Lee authoritatively, turning a page. "Your odds are just fine."

Isabel feels vastly reassured. Lee, the bookie's daughter, knows how the world really works: there are rungs that can be grasped and held; there are laws; there are odds that can be calculated, bets that can be won. Lee's pajamas are soft; her skin is soft. Isabel notices that the skin along Lee's hipbone is just the tiniest bit looser than it used to be, although her thighs are still strong, with those long runner's curves of muscle that feel like bones. Lee used to run quite a bit, before her knees gave out. Isabel plucks gently at the skin over her own hip, pats Lee's flat stomach. Lee smells of the blue oil she adds to her bath, thick stuff with a delicate, warm scent that settles over them both like a veil.

"I thought of leaving you today," says Isabel.

"Yeah," says Lee, yawning. "I thought of leaving you, too." Lee closes her book, reaches up to snap out the light. "Isabel." She turns over, drawing Isabel into her, closing her arms around Isabel and kissing her on the shoulder. "Go to sleep."

Lee, around her, is the sea, rising and falling. Isabel, the lazy rowboat, floats there, dreamy, exhausted. The day, the dress, Thea, all begin to recede, to drift away, as Isabel casts them off, just as she cast off her rings a few minutes before, tossing each one into the old green box on the dresser, the one with the leaves carved into the side. She tries to count: how many of those rings were ones that Lee gave her? And for what occasions? Meanwhile, Lee — and this is always her way, especially when she's been mad, why is Isabel surprised, it's as if she never stops playing hide and seek with herself — Lee is slowly lifting Isabel's tank top with one warm hand, pushing it up Isabel's back and then putting her tongue where her hand has just been. As Lee's tongue moves up her spine, Isabel seems to herself to grow taller, deeper, stronger, more sure. Lee slides both hands through the enormous armholes of Isabel's top to cup her breasts, find the nipples first with her fingers, then, turning Isabel over, with her mouth, pulling at one, then the other, like something seeking nourishment.

Who is the baby now? thinks Isabel suddenly, unbuttoning Lee's pajama top as Lee arrives on top of her, kissing her on the mouth, pulling Isabel's tank top off and now there is nothing between them, it is just their flesh meeting everywhere, Lee's leg pushing between Isabel's legs.

Not yet.

Isabel rolls Lee over and slides her hand in between Lee's legs, slides her thumb deep inside, then scrunches down in the bed to get at Lee's clit with her tongue and feel her open. *Who is the baby now?* Isabel strokes Lee's small breasts, warm coins, then all nipple, and there is the tiny scar under her right breast — it was nothing, a benign mole — like that same field with the horse in it you always see on the last curve toward home, and somehow the field with the horse looks different each time, as if it is telling the time — Lee opening, Isabel, scrunched down in the bed, opening, the constant pull and tug between them, the constant demand: more.

There is never enough, never, not in all the time in the world. Lee comes, and comes, and comes, each one traveling down through Isabel's tongue like an echo in her own body, stronger than any sound or motion of the flesh. It is almost as if she is coming herself or having a memory, or a premonition, of coming, as the other's movement slams through her, rocking her inside and out. *Who is the baby now?*

There is a pause. Isabel slithers up, kisses Lee's hip, presses her lips, her tongue, to the slope of skin there. It is sweet. Lee, her hair damp along her forehead, pulls Isabel on top of her, draws her hand right down through the center of Isabel and the feeling goes through Isabel like a shot; her fingers are warm; her thighs are warm. Isabel is three seconds away. She hovers on top of Lee, but it feels like Lee is somewhere above, pulling her up.

After, they lie side by side on the bed, too sweaty to embrace yet, to do more than simply touch their pinkies together like two girls who have had the same thought at the same moment and nod silently to one another *I know.* Isabel draws the sheet up, everything exquisitely cool and warm at the same time, air and bedclothes and the scent of the two of them all interlaced.

She falls asleep.

Morning

Isabel wakes up alone to the sound of a faint fall breeze rattling the window in its old frame. She leans over from the bed and turns off the air conditioner, uncertain for a moment what day it is. Her tank top and Lee's pajamas are tangled on the floor by a corner of the bed. One of Lee's many eyeglass cases, the tortoiseshell one, is lying open on the nightstand, near her Mob book which looks about to fall. Isabel snaps the case shut but leaves the bed unmade, the nightclothes on the floor, the book at its perilous angle. She reaches into the closet for her bathrobe. The black-purple sheath of her dress is sticking out; she straightens it on the hanger and slides it back into the overfull closet with the others. There is Lee's chipped white teacup on the dresser. There is Isabel's little notebook on the windowsill, just where she left it. In the other room is the rustle of Lee, the ching of the toaster oven, the murmur of NPR explaining that the world has really changed very little since yesterday. Isabel thinks how lucky she is, leaning against the dresser, sipping cold tea. It's Friday. Yesterday was Thursday. Everything is fine. This is the way life goes: just when you think you're headed for the cliff, etc. It was so smoky in The Rack, so silly, everyone with their little plastic cups of white wine in the dark, Thea leaning in to kiss her in that oddly frank way: *So here it is. Do you like it?* But the cliff is an illusion, the cliff is the sadness of the past, a single frame of film, burning to white. Thea's hair smelled of the bar and there was an acrid taste in her mouth Isabel didn't quite like. Thea was too short or Isabel was too tall; they shifted, but couldn't seem to find a position that fit. And then the kiss was over. They parted, looked at each other. What was there to say? Thea turned away and disappeared into the crowd, which reseamed behind her.

Isabel sips the cold tea. This is what's real. The ching of the toaster oven, the murmur of NPR, IBM going up or down. Frida Kahlo's water-splashed eyebrows. In the other room the teapot whistles its lonely tune and is stilled. She sees the number, faint but still entirely legible, inscribed in ballpoint on her palm. A little game of hands and telephone numbers from distant cities. She lowers her hand. She raises it again, finishing the tea. She wonders vaguely what to wear today, while on another floor a phone rings, a voice answers.

FORUM

Jianhua Road South, Beijing

Jianying Zha

THE STREET I GREW UP ON IN BEIJING didn't have a name until the 1980s. It used to be a small dirt road off the east end of Changan Avenue, Beijing's main east-west thoroughfare. When my family first moved there in the mid-60s, that whole area east of Jianguo Gate was considered Beijing's outskirt. The city ended abruptly here: the moment you turned off the main road you were in the middle of nowhere. Patches of cabbage and potato farm scattered here and there. An unpleasant stench of the outhouses and manure lingered in the air. Various mud lanes crawled across the field, leading to clusters of ramshackle cottages. On a rainy day, all the roads, including our street, turned into yellow slosh, and people had to wear their rubber boots to go out.

But my family felt almost euphoric about the move. Until then, we had been living at the heart of the old imperial capital, Root of the Royal City, inside a large traditional courtyard compound built in the late Qing dynasty as an occasional dwelling place for Li Lianying, a celebrated, powerful eunuch favored by the Empress Dowager. It was confiscated after the communist victory in 1949 and distributed to the staff of the new municipal government, where both of my parents worked in the 50s. With six connected courtyards, various gardens and trees, the compound was enormous and very elegant, but sharing it among a hundred families inevitably turned it into a crowded place. Our family received only two rooms, had to get water from the well in the yard, cook on a small coal-burning stove and use a communal outhouse. The high-ceilinged rooms in winter would turn into a cold, dank and dark igloo. The shuddering of the windows on Beijing's windy nights accompanied the dreams of my early childhood; the outdoor water pipes would freeze solid in the mornings.

So when my father finally transferred to the Chinese Academy of Social Sciences, which gave him a four-room unit in a row of brand-new apartment buildings, my parents rejoiced. The move also took on a symbolic meaning for them because it seemed to signal the end of their political travails since the anti-rightist campaign. It didn't matter that we were now on the city's outskirt, we had a better home to ourselves: bigger, brighter, more modern — for the first time we had our own kitchen, bathroom and central heating! This was an infinitely more desirable place than the old one we left behind.

THE AREA, GENERALLY REFERRED TO as "Outside the Jianguo Gate," was just beginning to be developed. In imperial times it had fallen outside the walls of the old Tartar City, though the Temple of the Sun, a landmark of the region set within its own great somber enclosure, was a place for important annual court ceremonies. But the entire old Peking, capital for several dynasties over seven hundred years, whose grand design was an architectural wonder that enamored westerners like Marco Polo, was subjected to a complete transformation in the hands of Mao. In the name of modernization and copying a plan directly from

Moscow, the communist government launched a relentless campaign to change Beijing into an industrial center and a monumental symbol for the socialist state. Ancient city walls and gates were torn down, subways and factories were built, streets were widened and concrete buildings went up. The speed of destruction and construction was such that by the mid-60s, the claustrophobic, romantic splendor of the old city had largely vanished; on its ashes rose the beginning of a more open, dull and, yes, modern city.

In this new "grand design," the capital was to fan out in all directions, and satellite towns were to be planted like so many bright stars surrounding the red sun. Our little region on the east side, humble and barren as it appeared then, would therefore fall handily within the newly expanded city perimeter. Already, a lumber factory was moving in, and various housing projects were under way. In fact, precisely because it was virtually empty ground, it stood the best chance of becoming the most "modern." As the Chairman once famously noted: "It is easy to draw the newest and most beautiful picture on a blank sheet of paper."

So, fervent believers in modernization, my parents sighed with satisfaction about our new home and were optimistic about the future of this developing neighborhood. My father's contentment was slightly dampened when it was found that our hot-water tap over the bathtub delivered no hot water, and for that matter, no cold water either. "A piece of decoration like a deaf man's ear," he grumbled, fidgeting wistfully with the unresponsive tap that would remain absolutely dry for the ensuing twenty-some years. But at least all the cold-water taps worked fine. My mother couldn't get over how wonderfully the toilet flushed — a wonder indeed, since nine out of ten Chinese toilets don't flush properly and ours, by the way, broke down within a fortnight and since then was never quite able to recreate its initial miraculous performance. Still, these were tiny imperfections in an immensely improved larger picture.

But as a small child I felt ambivalent about this new neighborhood. From our fourth-floor balcony the general surroundings looked bare, drab, our nameless street an empty, cheerless mud line. I missed our charming old courtyard with its many cozy, intriguing nooks and crannies — excellent for playing hide-and-seek, or listening to the old man down the lane playing sad folk tunes on his *erhu*. How good it was to be able to just walk out of one's door into a gracefully contained world of nature. How much fun it had been on those leisurely weekends to go with my parents to a market or to a park with lotus-draped lakes and hump-back stone bridges — all within easy reach from our old home. And much as I enjoyed our larger interior space, I didn't like being cooped up in a tall concrete box. Of course, at that age I knew nothing about the ancient Chinese folk fear of losing contact with *diqi*, the spirit from the earth, which my parents would dismiss as superstition; yet my discomfort with being "propped up in mid-air" was more than a simple childish fear of height. The train whistles (Beijing Railway Station was not so far from us now) sounded awfully lonesome at night, and I noted with dismay that no dog's bark could be heard from here.

SOON ENOUGH THOUGH, MY PARENTS' HOPES for the neighborhood were dashed. In 1966, the Cultural Revolution broke out, whipping up all Chinese energies into a vicious political frenzy. In the ensuing fifteen years our street suffered a sort of stunted development, as did the entire region, which froze into a skeleton outpost of Maoist-style modernity. Rows of apartment buildings stood in neat order, with minimal service structure and even less signs of real neighborhood life. The one and only small state-run restaurant that managed to open up on our street, for example, had exactly the same miserable menu scribbled on a blackboard all through my adolescent years. The street was pitch-black after sunset.

Meanwhile, political storms raged on our little street. Mass parades, hysterical rallies, giant slogans painted across building walls denouncing the scholars and intellectuals living in them — a couplet against my parents brushed across our first-floor entrance glared at me for years. Yet no one ever bothered to pave the dirt road, fix the potholes or the broken garbage chute. Because of my parents' renewed political trouble, I dreaded walking through the nearby workers' apartment complex on the way to school, because some mean-spirited kids there always chased me with stones. But when I visited a couple of my classmates' homes there, it was clear that, despite their superior class status, the workers lived in even worse material conditions than ours, with paint peeling off the darkened walls of their smaller, more shoddy units.

The only new piece of construction on our street during those dark years took place in the mid-70s. It was the Friendship Store, a three-story department store standing by the intersection of Changan Avenue and our street. In those days of strict rationing (rice, sugar, cooking oil, everything), this brightly lit place with all sorts of rare consumer items for foreigners only looked like a mirage in a desert. Of course the only time I stepped inside was before its completion, when my middle school organized us to help the workers. As soon as the store opened, no local residents were allowed to go near its guarded tall glass doors.

BY THE MID-80S I WAS LIVING IN THE UNITED STATES and one day a letter from my parents informed me that a street name had finally been added to our home address. It was Jianhua Road South. Jianhua means "Build China."

Now, naming a street with a slogan reminds me unpleasantly of a popular Cultural Revolution practice (many Chinese streets today still have names that shout absurd battle cries at you), but in the 80s China was being built up in a rather different direction than before. The economic and political reforms so lifted people's spirits that there was a genuine atmosphere of rejuvenation. Every time I returned to Beijing I was impressed by the changes. My father, forever the optimist, never skipped a chance to point out all the new hotels and commercial buildings springing up in our district. "The situation is very good," he'd confidently conclude. To him, the country was back on track under Deng, and this time around we'd have a more humane modernization.

He was to die the year after the Tiananmen massacre, a shock from which he never fully recovered. But China moved on after a brief halt. The buildup picked up again in the 90s, the pace dizzying. Beijing often felt like a giant construction site: new skyscrapers, new roads, rubble and junk everywhere, red cranes going up, brown dust settling down. Our area, Outside the Jianguo Gate, has turned into a bustling, glittering new commercial center with many upscale hotels, businesses and shopping plazas.

Each time I visited, Jianhua Road South took on a more prosperous look, along with all the noise and chaos. The street was dug up constantly: to lay new pipes, to widen, to repave. One after another, restaurants, fruit stalls, clothes vendors, music stores, karaoke bars and newsstands lined up on both sides. Day and night, the street was full of sounds and dust: people on bicycles, vegetables in carts, construction material on trucks, migrant laborers and office clerks on lunch break, slick businessmen on cellular phones and taxicabs weaving through the crowd, honking and scraping elbows. There is even a stock-trading center now, right opposite our building. The old plain state-run restaurant on the block was first renovated, then torn down, then replaced by a Peking Duck chain and most recently transformed into a joint-venture Brazilian Grill. Getting too exotic? Well, it's got to compete with neighbors across the road like Manhattan and Taipei Breakfast King.

YET WHILE I CHEER HEARTILY FOR THE BELATED ARRIVAL of a measure of "the good life" in our neighborhood, the phantom of history has always lurked just around the corner. It creeps up in uncanny ways. By a fish stall in our neighborhood's cheerfully overstocked farmers' market, my mother once ran into a man with a familiar face: he turned out to be a leader who had ransacked our home during the Cultural Revolution. "Do you remember who I am?" asked my mother. "Aren't you the one who hit me?" The man paled, looked guilty for a moment, then hurried away to buy a fish; she was slowing him down in getting his fish. Sometimes, when I turned off busy Changan Avenue into our busy street, the sound of tanks rolling by and a crowd of cursing residents gathered on the sidewalks would abruptly come on, as though a silent walkman were suddenly turned on, louder than the din of all the lively pushing and selling before my eyes.

Rush, rush, rush. This is the speed on our street: too many precious years lost, too little time to waste now, and two more years the millenium will be gone. *Xiang qian kan. Xiang qian kan.* Look ahead. Look at the money. This is the attitude that saves the day. Will it save the night too? How long can we go on with this play?

Let us only pray.

WORDS

There is no ambiguity about the term diaspora when it is used in relation to the Jewish people.
— The Penguin Atlas of Diasporas

Whoever lives in Babylon is considered as though living in the Land of Israel.
— Talmud

"There's more Jewish heart at the knish counter at Zabar's than in the whole of the Knesset!"
— ZIAD, *Philip Roth's Palestinian friend, in* Operation Shylock

"DIASPORA"

Alisa Solomon

AMONG THE MOST TRIUMPHALIST PRONOUNCEMENTS made by Bibi Netanyahu during Israel's much ballyhooed jubilee celebrations this spring was his prediction that within the next several years Israel will become home to a majority of the world's Jews. More than the declaration of the state in 1948, more than the capture of additional territory in the 1967 war, more than the continued expropriation of Palestinian land through the 70s, 80s and 90s, more than the expansion of Jewish settlements in the Occupied Territories even after the signing of the Oslo peace accords in 1993, even up to this moment — more than all these geographic conquests, this demographic fact heralded the fulfillment of Zionism's fondest dream: the peopling of the land with Jews (or, to use the Israeli government's own term, the "Judaizing" of the land). And more than that, the ingathering — or at least the outstripping — of the Diaspora.

In making this claim, Netanyahu was quick to note that had the Hebrews never been dispersed from *Eretz Yisroel* 3,000 years ago, we would number some 120 million by now — ten times our current global population. If only we'd stayed where we belonged, he seemed to suggest, as if commenting on a kid who had disobediently strayed beyond the backyard just before supper time instead of on several millennia of worldwide wanderings, nothing bad would have happened to us. Netanyahu didn't explicitly mention the Holocaust. But then the Holocaust goes without saying when Zionism is asserting its supremacy over Diaspora.

Careful not to alienate his supporters among American Zionists — those Jews, as the old joke goes, who are willing to pay other Jews to live in Israel for them — Netanyahu hastened to add, "It is not the idea of a diaspora. Other peoples have their diasporas. The Chinese have a diaspora, a far-flung diaspora, but they have a coherent center. We lost the coherent center and were dispersed."

But now, Netanyahu crowed, in that peculiar Israeli admixture of secular nationalism and messianic assurance, the center would hold. Coherence would be restored because Israel's Jewish population had amassed as naturally as dunes forming in the windblown desert sands — never mind elaborate efforts over the last five decades to import Jews from Northern Africa, the Arab states, Russia, Ethiopia and the former Soviet republics, nor early government incentives for Jewish women to produce many children. At last, the Jewish state would assert its moral authority by boasting that the Chosen People had chosen the Land. At last, Zionism would have a statistical rationale for its ascendant assumptions. After a century of deriding Diaspora — in the excessive effort to produce tough new Jews — Zionism could proclaim that the Diaspora needed it more than it needed the Diaspora. (Indeed, more U.S. dollars flow to Israel from evangelical Christians than from American Jews; in Congress, it's the politicians most aligned with the Christian Right who pay greatest fealty to the Israeli right.)

OUTSIDE THE HOLY LAND, DIASPORA is a trendy neighborhood in these days of post-colonial studies. Everyone seems to want to live there. There's a catchy, even queer cachet to the word nowadays, as it has been called on to describe transnational, hybrid groups of people who can be both appealingly non-patriotic and authentically multiculti, drawing their identity from a homeland left behind but never forgotten. Replacing more narrow, specific terms like "Overseas Chinese" or the "Irish migration," diaspora promises multidirectional movements of people, cash and ideas. And in some cases, at least, like pre-Zionist Jewish diaspora, it connotes a non-territorialist sense of nationhood that troubles the hoary hegemony of the nation-state. Diaspora, in sum, posits virtual community over "imagined community."

Indeed, diaspora is an especially useful term in this information age as the Internet enables an efficient, expansive analogue to those trade networks Jews built across Europe in the early modern era. Ever since the Tiananmen Square massacre, Overseas Chinese from all corners of the globe have been e-mailing each other to organize mass support for democracy; an Irish fiddler in Sydney downloads riffs from her landsman in Boston. Some theorists even talk about a queer diaspora — gay and lesbian kids eagerly poring over the pages of *Out* in their garages in Illinois or blaring k.d. lang on their Walkpersons in Montana before being ingathered to Chelsea or the Castro.

To be sure, diaspora is not all romance and peppy po-mo border transgression; it's often instigated by dispossession, war, famine, persecution. "Exile is strangely compelling to think about but terrible to experience," as Edward Said has suggested. "Its essential sadness can never be surmounted."

Unless, perhaps, the distance of millennia — not to mention a long tradition of figurative scripture reading — makes metaphor of the memory, as it did for Jews until the advent of Zionism a hundred years ago. Through the centuries, Jews lost the literal pull from *Eretz Yisroel*, like metal filings strewn too far from a magnet to be tugged toward it, yet they remained somehow charged with a sense of that insurmountable sadness. Over time, over space, melancholy attenuated into musing, and over the migrating ages, Jews mused their way into Modernism, Marxism, creative marginality. Only now, as the 50th anniversary celebrations of Israel's founding are winding down, and Netanyahu's hawkish recalcitrance is heating up, are American Jews beginning to recognize that Zionism took the poetry out of Jewish diaspora — even as it instigated, most literally, a violent diaspora for Palestinians.

Post-colonial theorists, then, appropriate diaspora at a dicey moment for its original designees. No doubt these theorists are drawn to the term for, among other things, the moral valences it collected as it was carried for thousands of years, like the hastily assembled baggage of the refugee, on the backs of Jews; at the same time, they hold out Israel as one of the few countries that hasn't yet put a "post" before its "colonialism." Metaphorically, Jews remain the markers of modernity as a condition of exile; in real life, the fact of Israel, along with Jewish economic and political success in America, expel us from the ragged edges of resistance that diaspora denotes in contemporary discourse.

THE JEWISH DIASPORA BEGAN with the Assyrian conquest of Israel in 722 B.C.E., and expanded when Nebuchadnezzar exiled the Judeans to Babylonia around 600 B.C.E. Even after a return to *Eretz Yisroel* was permitted two generations later, many Judeans elected to stay in Babylonia. And in another six centuries, after the Roman sacking of the Second Temple, Babylonia flourished as a center of Jewish population and culture. The Rabbinic tradition of this period sets in motion a productive diasporic dialectic between exile and return, often suggesting — notwithstanding the *Penguin Atlas of Diasporas*' claim that Jews know no ambiguity on this score — that life outside the Land could be as holy and fulfilling, as Jewish, as life inside. And even, maybe, that Jews could be more Jewish when living the Law in a strange land than when wielding power in their own. The longing for Zion expressed in the ever-evolving liturgy was often more a yearning for spiritual wholeness than for a particular chunk of real estate.

It's the very fact of diaspora that gives us the word: a Greek translation of the Hebrew Bible around 250 B.C.E. occasioned by Jewish dispersal throughout the Greek empire. It first appears when God warns the People Israel not to neglect God's law. If only they observe the commandments, they're told, among other blessings, "The Lord will give you abounding prosperity in the issue of your womb, the offspring of your cattle and the produce of your soil in the land that the Lord swore to your fathers to give you" (Deuteronomy 28:11). But if they do not, the People Israel will be subjected to a catalogue of some sixty horrific curses — among them, calamity, panic, frustration, consumption, fever, drought, madness, blindness, cuckoldry, robbery, locusts, kidnapping, starvation, "malignant and chronic diseases," "hemorrhoids, boil-scars and itch" and even "a severe inflammation from which you shall never recover — from the sole of your foot to the crown of your head." Among these magnificent maledictions comes a threat that seems far less dire given the context: "the Lord will scatter you among all the peoples from one end of the earth to the other" (Deuteronomy 28:64). The Hebrew, *v'hefitzekha* — you will be scattered, like seeds — is captured well in the Greek, *dia speirein* — to sow, by scattering. The image appears repeatedly throughout the Torah — and almost always as punishment.

It's the Prophets who introduce exile as a synonym for diaspora. To this day, the Hebrew word *galut* is used by Israelis to describe those stubbornly wayward Jews who haven't availed themselves of the Law of Return. Its hard-edged consonants and thumping iamb still bludgeon like a Biblical curse — even when wielded by folks who flock to the beaches of Tel Aviv on Yom Kippur.

But in its Yiddish pronunciation — *ga'-lus* — the word is a cushion, inviting a different kind of covenant. Yiddish, after all, is the language of landlessness, the babble of border crossing. It's the quintessential diasporic tongue, picking up phrases, vocabulary, alphabet, syntax from wherever Ashkenazi Jews touched down, its speakers spilling over the pesky perimeters of nation-states. Those rootless cosmopolitans we all now yearn to be spoke in its rounded tones. *Galus* was a good address.

TODAY, AMONG SOME YOUNG, LEFTY AND OFTEN QUEER Ashkenazi Jews in America, there's a heady return to *Yiddishkayt,* as if the grandchildren and great-grandchildren of the Lower East Side of yore are snatching post-colonial theory's ideas about diaspora to set their own story right. They reckon their people's exile not in the terms of some ancient tribal Bible story, but in the same terms as all the immigrants who have jumbled into the U.S. — in more recent traumas of ship holds, border patrols, refugee camps, labor demands and newly sprung hopes. (Would there even be a modern Israel, one can't help wondering, if the U.S. had kept its borders open in the early 20s?)

American Jews are a doubled diaspora. The diffuse, always already displaced center from which their forebears were dispersed two generations ago was annihilated and has become as mythic, as impossible to return to collectively, as *Eretz Yisroel* was for European Jews — at least until modern nationalism showed them how. But you don't have to call for the mass return of Ashkenazi Jews to Europe like the crazed diasporist posing hilariously as Philip Roth in *Operation Shylock* to want to dislodge Zionism from its claim as the core. You don't have to demonize Israel to recognize that when it comes to a Jewish American narrative of diaspora, the Bund bears more meaning than Babylon.

Indeed, it was the Bund — the secular socialist-democratic labor and cultural movement founded in Vilna in 1897 and spreading throughout Eastern Europe until being extinguished by the Holocaust — that articulated the most compelling alternative to Zionism. Drawing far more support among Eastern European Jewry than Herzl's project of mass emigration, Bundism was winning the debate until it was cut off in midsentence by Hitler. Unable to imagine the cataclysm Nazism and fascism would bring, Bundists maintained that Jews did not have to uproot *en masse* for the land of Palestine to fulfill their identity or find equality; they could achieve that by struggling, alongside non-Jews, for democracy and socialism in the places they already lived, while sustaining and developing their own language, literature and culture. That sense of being rooted in and obliged to bring justice in the place one inhabited was what Bundists called *doykayt* — here-ness. At once anti-assimilationist and internationalist, particular and universal, *doykayt* is Jewish diaspora's most radical bequest.

ZIONISM IS, NECESSARILY, ITS NEGATION. Undoubtedly, Israel has served as a haven for persecuted Jews, but Zionism's efforts to create facts on the ground has also privileged ingathering over assisting viable Jewish communities in the Diaspora. What's more, it zealously forged newcomers into a new Israeli identity, wiping out Ladino, Judeo-Arabic and Yiddish along with the cultural practices of their speakers. It's no contradiction that Israel Zangwill, whose maudlin 1908 melodrama popularized the term "melting pot" in the U.S., also came up with the specious Zionist slogan "a land without a people for a people without a land." Assimilation and nationalism both dissolve diaspora.

One of the most popular tourist attractions in Tel Aviv is the Diaspora Museum. The exhibition's richness and reach boggles the imagination, but the longer one walks among the display cases, the more the thrill gives way to dread. It's a commonplace that societies commemorate cultures in museums only when they are no longer vital, and one can't help feeling like a relative called into a morgue to identify a body as she walks past an illuminated *ketubah* from 16th-century Germany, a richly embroidered *tallis* from Morocco, an engraved silver *kiddush* cup from Vilna, *shabbos* candlesticks from Iraq.

If Netanyahu's numbers are right, perhaps Israel will stop trying to yank Jews in the *galut* into its borders. If not, as the last couple of elderly Bundists die and the Zionist end of the age-old dialectic is left as entirely uncontested as capitalism, anti-fundamentalist Jewishness here will face two distressing options: dissolving into an uninflected Americanness or making Zionism its religion — and only defining characteristic. But just maybe, once relieved of Israel's anxious tugging, American Jews will be able to make the Return that matters more: to that disaggregated, generative Jewish identity, that wandering and wondering consciousness that blooms, like a spray of wildflowers from scattered seeds, only in diaspora.

Sermons

Farah Jasmine Griffin

for Cornel and Tukufu

"Let me tell you about love, that silly word you believe is about whether you like somebody or whether somebody likes you or whether you can put up with somebody in order to get something or someplace you want or you believe it has to do with how your body responds to another body like robins or bison or maybe you believe love is how forces or nature or luck is benign to you in particular not maiming or killing you but if so doing it for your own good.

"Love is none of that. There is nothing in nature like it.... Love is divine only and difficult always. If you think it is easy you are a fool. If you think it is natural you are blind. It is a learned application without reason or motive except that it is God.

"You do not deserve love regardless of the suffering you have endured. You do not deserve love because somebody did you wrong. You do not

deserve love just because you want it. You can only earn — by practice and careful contemplation — the right to express it and you have to learn how to accept it. Which is to say you have to earn God. You have to practice God. You have to think God — carefully. And if you are a good and diligent student you may secure the right to show love. Love is not a gift. It is a diploma. A diploma conferring certain privileges: the privilege of expressing love and the privilege of receiving it.

"How do you know you have graduated? You don't. What you do know is that you are human and therefore educable, and therefore capable of learning how to learn, and therefore interesting to God, who is interested only in Himself which is to say He is interested only in love. Do you understand me? God is not interested in you. He is interested in love and the bliss it brings to those who understand and share that interest."

— Toni Morrison, *Paradise*

Reverend Senior Pulliam, the "prideful preacher" of Toni Morrison's latest novel *Paradise*, joins the ranks of other Morrison characters who offer sermons and meditations on love. There is the oft quoted sermon in the clearing by Baby Suggs in *Beloved*, Eva Peace's response to her daughter Hannah's question, "Did you love us?" in *Sula* and the silent deliberation of Pulliam's young foil in *Paradise*, Reverend Richard Misner.

Pulliam is one of the older founders of the fictional all black town of Ruby, Oklahoma. Following the failure of Reconstruction, the founders of Ruby joined large numbers of African Americans who sought freedom from racial violence and legal discrimination. They have built a prosperous and safe haven. For many of this generation, Ruby is indeed Paradise. For their children, it is an isolated island that refuses to enter into the tumultuous changing world of the Civil Rights and Black Power movements. Pulliam's sermon is offered at the wedding of two members of this younger generation, K.D. and Arnette. The wedding represents a reconciliation of two important families and a possible consolidation of the power that the founding generation wields.

The conflict between these two generations is evident in Pulliam's sermon as is his orthodox Calvinist theology. For Pulliam there is no birthright to Divine Love, there is no Guarantee — not even for a people who have had to wander constantly in search of safety, in search of home, who have experienced dispossession, displacement and dismemberment. This is no wedding celebration; instead, it is an admonition, a lecture and warning. Get rid of those silly, romantic notions you have about love. Get rid of that crazy idea you have picked up that God gives a damn about you. If you are lucky you might earn love but there is nothing you can do to deserve it. Deserve. In *Song of Solomon*, the selfish, spoiled young Milkman reflects on the word *deserve*. He first states it as something he takes for granted, then he questions it, and finally he implicitly compares it to the word *earn*. He grows up when he learns that he "deserves" nothing and must earn respect, love and manhood. However, in Pulliam's sermon, even after you learn the difference between deserve and earn, there is still no promise of God's interest in or love for you. Divine Love is the only love and it seems so very arbitrary in its selection. One thing is clear, it will not select a wayward and disobedient younger generation as long as they insist on challenging the status quo. For Pulliam and the other living founders, Ruby has been chosen. That is why its inhabitants so rarely die. Anyone or anything that challenges their interpretation of God's Divine Mission is likely to meet with His Wrath as manifested through them and their actions toward the infidels.

RICHARD MISNER IS A YOUNGER MINISTER of the church where the wedding is taking place. He is not a native of Ruby but an outsider chosen not by the elders of Ruby but by the mother church. He also supports and encourages the younger generation's visions, questioning of authority and, in some sense, their organized rebellion. Misner is supposed to help officiate over the wedding ceremony, but he is so angered by Pulliam's wounding words that he chooses to respond with a silent meditation on the cross and on its relationship to God's love for humanity. He carries the cross dramatically from its stand in the back of the church to the front, where all wedding guests, bride and groom and Pulliam himself can see.

The Christ on the cross of Misner's meditation guarantees Divine Love as a birthright of all human beings. "See? The execution of this one solitary black man propped up on these two intersecting lines to which he was attached in a parody of human embrace.... See? His woolly head alternately rising on his neck and falling toward his chest, the glow of his midnight skin dimmed by dust.... See how this official murder out of hundreds...moved the relationship between God and man from CEO and supplicant to one on one?" This black Christ is an ancestor figure of all the lynched and dismembered black men, those who are on death row and those who die at the hands of angry mobs; this Christ has suffered like and for everyone oppressed, particularly the black oppressed.

This silent sermon echoes those of the early Gnostic Christians, considered heretical by institutional religion. The political implications of Misner's theology threaten the orthodoxy of Pulliam, just as the Gnostics threatened the early church. The meditation begins and ends with a question — "See?" "Would they see? Would they?" It leaves it open and as such invites participation, refusing to be dogmatic and insisting on engagement. And it insists on the gift of Divine love, a gift purchased with the crucifixion:

> *The cross he held was abstract; the absent body was real, but both combined to pull humans from backstage to the spotlight, from muttering in the wings to the principal role in the story of their lives. This execution made it possible to respect — freely, not in fear — one's self and one another. Which was what love was: unmotivated respect. All of which testified not to a peevish Lord who was His own love but to one who enabled human love. Not for His own glory — never. God*

> *loved the way humans loved one another; loved the way humans loved themselves; loved the genius on the cross who managed to do both and die knowing it.*

If God loves the way human beings love each other, if love is unmotivated respect, then the elder generation of Ruby should give the same respect to the youth that they demand from them. They should meet all human beings, even those who challenge their way of life, on a common ground of respect. Misner's Christianity requires no intermediary, no institution to approach God on behalf of humanity; it requires of human beings only that they love and respect each other for in so doing they love and respect the Divine. This kind of love — the love for the Divine that must embody a love for all of creation — is not a simple love of pop songs but a deep, complex and difficult love. It is the love about which James Baldwin writes so often. The love that is connected to hope, not the hope of optimism but the hope of faith. Baldwin, particularly Baldwin of the essays in *The Fire Next Time*, is someone whose best work is situated in a love of the Divine and of humankind. Such work, novels, music, sermons that love and respect humanity as a form of Divine love, does not produce ideas that are destructive: from New World Slavery to modern genocides and ethnic cleansing.

WORK BASED IN A LOVE OF THE DIVINE and a love of humanity celebrates and enhances life. And, under the best of circumstances, weddings also celebrate and enhance life. However, unlike most sermons, performed to direct, guide and inform, this one is a silent one. Because Misner is so overcome with anger at Pulliam, he is unable to put his vision in a language that his congregates can understand. In his silence, he fails to do what the prophet is supposed to — communicate: "Richard Misner could not speak calmly of these things. So he stood there and let the minutes tick by as he held the crossed oak in his hands, urging it to say what he could not: that not only is God interested in you; He *is* you. Would they see? Would they?"

That question is answered by Morrison's providing glimpses into the thoughts of the wedding party and guests. All reflect on their own notions of love — ranging from the possessive, obsessive love of the groom for another woman to the bride's love that finds her losing all sense of herself to the beloved. Neither of these is the love of Pulliam or that of Misner. Only Billie Delia, the maid of honor and community outcast because of an early sexual transgression, has a complex notion of love. It seems she is also the only one to see what is meant by the two versions of love. The stalwart citizens of Ruby have only been judgmental of her, yet she has also been the recipient of unconditional love from the rogue women who all somehow end up living on the outskirts of town in a former convent. These women, who live independently without men and flaunt their sexuality, and feed themselves, offer yet another affront to the founding generation of Ruby. What Billie Delia also knows is that the struggle being waged between these two ministers is about something other than theology. She thinks to herself: "the real battle was...about disobedience, which meant, of course, the stallions were fighting about who controlled the mares and their foals."

The conflict identified by Billie Delia is essentially a generational conflict between the solid older citizens who founded Ruby and the younger ones who want the town to enter the world that is in the midst of social and political change. This conflict is as real and central as the one noted by most reviewers of the novel. Thus far critics have focused on the struggle between the men of the all black town (a racial utopia) and the unconventional women of the Convent (which some see as a feminist utopia). However, as Billie Delia, a member of Ruby's younger generation and a friend to the women of the convent, notes, the generational conflict is a struggle for the future of Ruby: "Senior Pulliam had scripture and history on his side. Misner had scripture and the future on his. Now, she supposed, he was making the world wait until it understood his position."

If Misner does in fact have the future on his side, he should have the gift of prophesy as well, but his failure to articulate his vision for his audience to embrace or reject puts in relief Morrison's own imperative to speak poetically and prophetically. As a poet she insists that readers contemplate the meanings of love — maternal love, romantic or erotic love, divine love — and so edges towards prophesy. She manages to heed Paul's command: "speaketh unto men to edification, and exhortation, and comfort" (1 Corinthians 14:3). What is the relationship between the poetry of Morrison's prose and her prophesy? Is there a distinction between the callings of poet and prophet, prophet and critic? For me, these are among the many questions raised by *Paradise*.

Harold Bloom, with whom I disagree in so many instances, sheds light upon the relationship between prophesy and poetry. *In Omens of Millennium: The Gnosis of Angels, Dreams, and Resurrection*, he distinguishes between "self-abnegating spirituality," which "always has been compatible with dogmatic orthodoxy in all the Western religions," and "self-affirming spirituality," whose lineage is just "as ancient and as honorable." "I think it no accident that the spirituality of the strong self has close affiliations with the visions of poets and people-of-letters.... Gnostics, poets, people-of-letters share in the realization of knowing that they know."

Pulliam espouses self-abnegating spirituality, Misner self-affirming spirituality. Both contrast sharply with the current obsession with somewhat self-serving 1–900 spirituality that is available to us through psychic hotlines, televangelists and appropriations of Native American, Eastern and various traditional African forms of spirituality. Here I am not trying to set up an easy distinction between institutionalized religion and New Age beliefs. Pulliam's sermon advocates a dedication to the human institution of a religion that controls and contains its members. Misner's sermon advocates a dedication to a form of spirituality that suggests that the Church only exists insofar as humans love each other. Both are ministers of an institutionalized religion. In our more secular society, people search for a more modern notion of spirituality, an attempt to locate meaning in their lives outside of institutions. Some of them turn to those things listed above.

SUCH A TENDENCY IS EVIDENCE OF OUR TIMES, the end of the 20th century when we have a myriad of texts and influences available to us. These are also convenient to the modern writer as well. Morrison's prophesy is informed by a range of influences not accessible to the Gnostics of early Christianity, helping her and her readers create one very important link between those of us who inhabit this age and the Gnostics: a radical openness to traditions, ideologies, thoughts, beyond those of our immediate context. We have a freedom to form our own concepts of spirituality, of meaning, of transcendence, because of the varied traditions offered us through scholarship, the media, technology and so on. In a modern urban secular society, the novel can be yet another canonical text in the construction of a spiritual practice.

In the past Morrison has said that her novels are an attempt to preserve and pass on the stories and the songs of the Black American past. As far as she is concerned, urbanization and integration have distanced Black Americans from the forms of knowledge previously available to them through their very distinctive culture. She has suggested that fiction can serve as a space of enlightenment, sustenance and renewal; it can serve to pass on values "of the tribe" much in the same way that black music and black religion as embodied in the sermonic tradition have.

Both music and sermons have served to transmit history and culture and articulate the conflicts, problems, visions and hope of Black Americans. They have provided a respite or a space of transcendence no matter how brief. In Morrison's fiction, specific sermons do this; sometimes the novels themselves attempt to do so. However, is it possible for contemporary black fiction to play the same role as the music and sermons, when they are read not only by black readers but by an international audience, when they are not performed within the context of black institutions but encountered in the very solitary practice of reading?

These differences make it difficult for novels to replace music and preaching in giving a sense of group identity and aspiration; however, they can be available as texts that seek to provide some discussion of the role of spirituality in navigating contemporary society. As an intellectual and a critic who is also a person of faith, I am somewhat envious of the room that creative writers have to take for granted the relationship between their spiritual, political and creative visions and practices. I have learned a great deal from them as I have from those early Gnostic Christians. Both have given me a sense of freedom by opening up possibilities for influence on my own work, politics and life.

AS IS THE CASE WITH MODERN SPIRITUALITY GENERALLY, I too have created my own eclectic and idiosyncratic selection of texts, influences, ancestors and saints. Certain encounters have always brought forth a feeling of transcendence from the mundane concerns of daily life for me, even as they involve those concerns. Such moments have almost always been encounters with music, literature, nature, political movements, romantic love, intense friendships, the ocean. Each of these in its own way has ushered me to what I imagined were also encounters with the divine. As a young girl, there was something about the music of Miles Davis and the prose of Toni Morrison that seemed to bring about a state of sublime transcendence — this at a time when church did not. While they since have been joined by other writers and musicians, Miles and Morrison are still most often my old standbys. For the past few years the space of friendship with individuals like my friend Salim Washington and my spiritual sister Imani Perry (musician/composer and thinker/writer respectively — might there be a pattern here?) and the voice of Cassandra Wilson have provided a kind of sacred space. Yes, the voice of Cassandra Wilson — jazz chanteuse, covergirl, interpreter of blues and pop.

You see, not so long ago I was in search of a retreat from an unwanted guest who had settled in for a long visit — Melancholia. Now I am not the first to seek escape from Melancholia through a retreat to spirituality; others have sought solace in drugs and alcohol. At first, the only thing that seemed to provide a temporary respite from my visitor were long walks in the park or by a river or ocean and listening over and over again to Cassandra Wilson's CD *New Moon Daughter*. Over and over again upon waking and then again as I courted sleep at night, Wilson's blue velvet voice would transport me from the blues which always awaited my return to wakefulness. As I pursued the path directed by that collection of songs, filled with its imagery of moons and water, I found myself variously consulting the Old Testament and that lovely orisha of the Seven Seas, Yemanja. Wilson's album seemed to insists upon this — but that is for another time, another essay.

In any case, a conversation about this quest with my friend, the artist Elizabeth King, led her to recommend Elaine Pagels' work to me, beginning with *The Gnostic Gospels*. After reading the introduction, I was hooked and began to read my way through her discussion of the history of early Christianity and the Gnostics. Pagels suggests that there is a strong resemblance between the Christ of the Gnostic Gospels and Buddha, so I began to read more about Buddhism. The writings of Thich Nhat Hanh, the Buddhist monk and author of *Living Buddha, Living Christ*, became very important to me for their willingness to engage creatively the teachings of Christ and Buddha, their commitment to social change and their insistent reminders to live a fully engaged life. Because Pagels asserts that the Gnostic Gospels include gospels written by women, I turned to one of them, *The Book of J* edited by Harold Bloom. But most importantly, Pagels led me to the Nag Hammadi, which took me back to Morrison, her colleague at Princeton.

THE NAG HAMMADI ARE COPTIC TRANSLATIONS of approximately "fifty-two texts from the early centuries of the Christian era — including a collection of early Christian gospels previously unknown." Pagels believes that these banned and buried texts "were part of a struggle critical for the formation of early Christianity." Much in these gospels asserts that to know oneself is to know God. This is an assertion that has been considered heretical throughout the history of institutionalized Christianity.

I first heard of the Nag Hammadi thanks to Morrison's *Jazz* and Julie Dash's film *Daughters of the Dust*. The epigraph of *Jazz* comes from "Thunder, Perfect Mind" of the Nag Hammadi:

> *I am the name of the sound*
> *and the sound of the name.*
> *I am the sign of the letter*
> *and the designation of the division.*

And Dash's luscious film opens with the voiceover, also quoted from "Thunder, Perfect Mind":

> *For I am the first and the last.*
> *I am the honored one and the scorned one.*
> *I am the whore and the holy one.*
> *I am the wife and the virgin....*
> *I am the barren one,*
> *and many are her sons...*
> *I am the silence that is incomprehensible...*
> *I am the utterance of my name.*

Such sweet language, such all-encompassing imagery, such possibility for the relationship between all that has come before and all that follows, between humans and God, such an expansive spirituality from two artists who hale from a group that has had its very humanity denied, who many have insisted are farthest from God. I have never heard the words of the Nag Hammadi from the mouths of any of the preachers I have encountered in person, but I have heard reflections of them in the preachers I have encountered in print, in the words particularly of those writers who for me are prophets, writers such as Morrison, who use literature to insist eloquently and consistently that we delve into the meanings and possibilities of love.

I don't believe in an interventionist God
But I know, darling, that you do.
— Nick Cave

The Labyrinth of Accusation

John Brenkman

As the credits and the last scene of Robert Duvall's *The Apostle* finished, the theater empty of everyone except those who make a habit of watching all the way through the music credits, I turned to Ben and said, Don't ever say I never took you to church.

We had been tiptoeing around a discussion of religion for several months, wary perhaps that it would be contentious and divisive. My remark was flip, and the anxieties it masked took a while to show themselves. Ben is now, at twenty, taking a close look at religion, attending Mass occasionally with his girlfriend and her family and reading books on belief and spirituality. My unease stemmed in part from having taught him so little about religion. My sons were spared a religious upbringing but were also, unjustifiably I have come to feel, deprived of a religious education.

The deeper unease, and source of our shying away from the topic, was that we had just had several conflict-ridden discussions about moral values in relationships and marriage. Ben was questioning choices I had made and disputing my explanations. He was also anxious about the difficulties that changes in my life were creating for him. Would he be to blame if he couldn't make all the adjustments he was facing? He said, It's like someone throwing you a plate. If you drop it and it breaks, whose fault is it? He then looked me in the eye and said, You've thrown me a lot of plates, Dad.

Our talk turned to the longer history of plates he has caught, including his mother's and my divorce, which he had seemed uncannily to take in stride when he was barely five, and the upheavals each of us had gone through when I moved away when he was twelve. We both revealed things that shocked the other. Our talks were honest and hard and painfully inconclusive. We both came away shaken and with a sharpened sense that there was much in our respective moral outlooks that diverged.

Ben's challenges were judgmental but not moralistic, for they sincerely arose from his own ongoing effort to express and validate the values he wants to live by. It remained implicit as we talked that religion — along with his discovery of the important role it played in another family — was crucially a part of his search for an ethic of relationships. The conflict between us made the question of belief too hot to handle for the moment. And I sensed that his current perception of my life as a whole made my nonbelief the backdrop or dogma or absence against which he was asking what to believe.

IN THE WAKE OF THESE EXCHANGES, I realized that while I have helped convey to my sons a thoroughly secular vision of the world and thoroughly secular values, I did not share with them the role religion itself centrally played in my own route to nonbelief. After a childhood of attending Sunday school, usually irregularly, at various easygoing, middle-class Presbyterian churches, I suddenly took the religious teachings to heart when I went through confirmation classes at fourteen. I avidly embraced the faith, spurred on by reading the Bible, religious tracts and doctrine and (considerably softened) accounts of the role of Luther and Calvin in the Reformation. It was a period of intense religious conviction that came tumbling down within a year as my readings and discussions took a rationalistic and atheistic turn. My loss of faith followed a common pattern: thrilling enlightenment and angry disillusion.

My nonbelief deepened, but my attitude toward it eventually changed, most decisively from reading the work of the philosopher Paul Ricoeur. Ricoeur's intent was to break down the dichotomy between reason and faith, the dichotomy in which my own loss of faith and secular convictions had first formed. He did not ask: does God exist? But rather: what are the symbols, narratives and discourses through which believers *experience* the existence of God? His question, it seemed to me, held for nonbelievers too. Just as theologians got stuck trying to prove the existence of God, nonbelievers usually get stuck trying to choose between the suspect certitudes of atheism and the timid hedging of agnosticism. The question lies elsewhere. I experience the nonexistence of God, and that experience is maintained through a range of ambiguous symbols, narratives and discourses which are my "equipment for living." From that standpoint, belief and nonbelief are both forms of belief. To believe there is no God is the same order of experience as believing there is one.

Religious and secular morality crisscross far more than we usually admit, and the admixtures follow no set pattern. Contemporary Christianity runs the gamut from fundamentalism to liberation theology and so connects faith to thoroughly contradictory moral premises, ethical principles and social aims. As for the confident expectations of Enlightenment atheists, whose rationalism provided the style of my own loss of faith as a teenager, the secularizing force of modernity has not rendered religion obsolete at all; religions grow worldwide as a response to modern life itself and often as a power politics.

Nonbelievers have to face an even more important fact of the crisscrossing of the sacred and the profane: there simply are no purely secular moralities. The genealogy of morals — of the symbols, maxims and feelings of moral experience — reaches "back" into religious traditions. The reverberations of past belief still speak in all our moral languages. Christianity casts wrongdoing as sin, and the Christian experiences sin as a need for redemption. Secular morality has to answer the challenge of understanding how people inevitably do harm and injury to one another. It tries to address this essential fallibility of social and interpersonal life, to assess the forms and meaning of injury, the experience of harming and being harmed, the demands of answerability and responsibility — all without appeal to an ultimate source of reconciliation.

WATCHING *THE APOSTLE* WAS THE MOST ENGAGING LOOK at religious experience Ben and I have shared. It wasn't a bad place to start, for the film itself puts the secular and the sacred uncomfortably in the same space. Robert Duvall (writer, director, star) creates in the figure of Sonny a southern Holy Roller preacher, entrepreneur, womanizer and felon, a man who uses his masculine swagger to give his ministry charisma just as he uses it to charm, persuade or intimidate the people around him. Much of the film is in fact like going to church — from the opening scene of a blind preacher in a tiny rural black church rhythmically pounding out the refrain "Nails in His feet for you and I," through Sonny's performances on the circuit with his Holy Ghost Power revivals, to the long sequence at the end in which he preaches and shouts and leads his congregation through spirituals, testimonials and a conversion before surrendering to the state troopers who have come to arrest him for murdering his wife's lover.

This dramaturgy of salvation is gripping and as likely to unsettle a believer as a nonbeliever, for Duvall's intent goes well beyond staging evangelical worship. Sonny's preaching is set in the thick of his troubled life. Yet the film is not a study of religious hypocrisy, either. Rather, it shows religious belief shaping a life and the life shaping the beliefs. *The Apostle* fulfills a thoroughly secular aesthetic imperative; it's a good movie because it dramatizes how a character, equipped with the unique design of his beliefs, symbols and values, shapes his acts and faces his fate.

In Sonny's case, this equipment for living takes its design from his religious faith. When events bend to his will, he is certain the Lord is leading him. When they confound it, he feels himself to be wrestling demonic powers, uncertain whether they lie within or outside him. Sonny's passions are violent and possessive, and the entire story is driven by his uninterrupted willfulness. When he discovers that his wife Jessie (Farrah Fawcett) is having an affair with Horace — the "puny-assed youth minister" — he first terrorizes them and then confronts Jessie in a scene filled with prayer and menace. As she sits on the sofa unloading his gun, she tells him, "I just want out of all this, that's all." He threatens to expose her affair, and she retorts that she knows all about "what you do and have done." He admits to his "wandering eye and weak and wicked ways," but affirms his love for her and tries to force her to pray with him for a reconciliation. She refuses: "my knees are worn out from praying with you." Sonny storms out, only to learn that Jessie has already orchestrated his ouster from the church.

Sonny lives his jealousy and rage as a spiritual crisis, for he is unhinged from the certainty his faith always gives him when he knows the meaning of what he does and what is done to him. In a riveting scene, he spends the night yelling at God. "I'm mad at you, Lord. I don't know who's been fooling with me, you or the devil." He acknowledges he is "a sinner once in a while, a womanizer," but appeals to the Lord for some word because they have always been "Jesus and Sonny" to each other. "Give me a sign or something," he pleads. "Blow it out of me. Give me peace." The depth of his crisis is revealed in the very fact that no sign comes; as the Lord stays silent, Sonny hurls himself into the film's two most explosive scenes.

First, he arrives at the church — "They can vote me out, but they can't lock me out. These people love me." — and struts in, decked out in his three-piece white suit and sunglasses, captivating the congregation as the choir sings "He's all right" and Jessie plays the keyboard. He dances around to Horace, stuffing a hundred dollar bill in his pocket and kissing him on both cheeks and then struts out, laying his hand on a woman's forehead (she faints). The swagger and mockery are flawless but empty; Jessie controls the church. His rage and a pint of whiskey take him next to the church camp baseball game, where, like a Homeric warrior tracking down the female spoils, he grabs Jessie by the hair and tries to force her and the children to go with him. When she resists, he picks up a baseball bat and knocks Horace unconscious — and flees.

The wrong is done, and this turning point in the film marks a decisive encounter between profane and sacred meanings, sharpening the potential conflict between Sonny's moral-symbolic world and the spectator's. He committed his crime feeling oppressed by rage and confusion and cut off from his God. In explaining to his friend Joe what has happened, he exhibits more righteousness than remorse: "I done it this time. Well, I let that sucker have it. I beat him like a one-legged stepchild. He may be on the road to glory this time." After ditching his car in a lake and throwing away all his identification, he stands one morning waist deep in a river and rebaptizes himself. He asks "permission to be accepted as an apostle of our Lord" and christens himself "without witnesses" the Apostle E.F. The clash of meanings is stark. For there is no difference between the Apostle's rebaptism and the fugitive's assumption of an alias; Sonny's exodus is life on the lam, his renewed dedication to walking a "straight line forever" with the Lord a flight from prosecution. Secure in his relation to his personal savior — "Once you're saved it's a done deal" — he goes where the Lord leads him, to Bayou Boutté, Louisiana, to preach again and build his One Way Road to Heaven church.

THE QUESTION THE FILM POSES in these scenes is not whether Sonny should have fled or stayed to face the consequences of his action. It is a question, rather, of his experience of accusation and blame and of the symbols in which that experience is cast. God and Satan are monsters of the absolute in fundamentalism's melodrama, and Sonny's language, private and public, is filled with the purifying symbolism of Good and Evil. The sacred permeates the film as the language in which Sonny interprets all that happens to him. *The Apostle* is drama not melodrama, however, and Duvall leaves pointedly unanswered the question posed by Horace's death: does Sonny ever see his violence as anything other than a jealous husband's righteous act of laying claim to what is rightfully his?

It is not in these terms that Sonny poses the question of his wrongdoing, but according to the design and idiom of his faith. Fleeing his crime, he says, "Satan has driven a big wedge between me and my family." And when he learns that his Mama is dying and he cannot return to be with her, he says, "Gettin' back at me, Lord, ain't you?" — as though his mother's suffering and death were God's retribution against *him*. These are the metaphors through which he feels accusation and punishment.

To say they are metaphors is not to say they are false. Ricoeur is clarifying here, for he has written with great insight on the experience of accusation, its centrality to the cultural and psychological foundations of morality. The Enlightenment tradition, from Kant to Freud, has tried to solve the conundrum of conscience: that blaming voice within ourselves which is mysteriously the voice of another — or an Other. Even the most secular explanations attribute conscience to some patently symbolic source: superego, parental authority, "community." Moral experience, as Ricoeur argues, is inescapably symbolic. The pure and the impure, captivity and exodus, sin and redemption — all these fundamental experiences of evil and the surpassing of evil are metaphorical. They are not simply draped in symbolism; we *live* the symbols, in the sense that our moral experience is inseparable from the metaphors and narratives through which we apprehend harm and the overcoming of harm.

What fascinates me about Robert Duvall's Sonny is that his experience of faith is so different from my own and yet is made accessible to understanding — to interpretation — through its symbolic unfoldings in the drama. In setting Sonny's symbolisms of evil over against his actions, Duvall discloses the all-too-human lineaments of the redeemed sinner. Sonny designates himself a sinner and feels himself redeemed, but how fully does he recognize his responsibility for the things he has done?

Nowhere is this question more forcefully raised than in the scene which most complexly explores the psychology and symbolism of accusation. The scene occurs the night before Sonny's rebaptism. As he lies with his Bible on his chest and a picture of Jessie and the children pinned to his tent, awaiting a sign to point his way, there is a voiceover of Jessie confessing her sins: "I feel as though I have crucified Christ afresh in what I have done. Adultery is a demonic possession. Once one has nullified the work of the cross, iniquity sets in. I am chagrined at my sin.... Forgive us our deeds and let us carry on your work, in the name of our Lord, Jesus Christ." This confession of course is not Jessie's inner monologue at all, but what Sonny imagines her confessing. His accusations against her come back to him in the voice of her abject repentance for wronging him. Having committed his crime in the dead space where he could not hear the Lord, he now hears the meaning of betrayal and loss in the form of what he wants Jessie to say, on the shadowy border between imagination and delusion. He needs her to speak these words to set his own moral universe right and give his own deeds their rightful place: he is the freshly slain Christ more than the wayward sinner, as though the iniquity that has set in — not only his ouster from the church but his own violence and separation from his children — sprung from her sin alone. In the course of the night he tears her head from the picture he has pinned up.

The path of accusation twists inside out, dispelling his confusions by demonizing her. The paths of accusation are always twisted, the labyrinth in which we have to discover in the inner and outer voices of blame what we are responsible for and answerable to. Sonny's demonization of Jessie opens anew for him the path to salvation; the next morning he becomes the born-again-again Apostle E.F. And so Duvall leaves another question pointedly unanswered: does Sonny's delivery into divine redemption turn on his refusal of a merely human responsibility?

THE REDEMPTIVE PROMISE OF CHRISTIANITY has increasingly taken the form, especially in contemporary Protestantism, of an affirmative religion of love. "For God so loved the world, that he gave his only begotten Son, that whosoever believeth in him should not perish but have everlasting life," according to John 3:16 and the banners that proselytize at public events from baseball games to anti-abortion rallies. Jesus died that we might live. In Sonny's preaching, the promised redemption is sweet, but God's love is even more fearsome than his retribution in its beyond-the-human extremity. At his last church service, Sonny takes a plump, happy baby from its mother's arms and, holding it up, exhorts his congregation to imagine driving nails through its soft tiny hands and into a board: "I don't have this much love in me to do this to my son, but God does."

The violence God let be done to his Son is the literal crux of Christian redemption. Whether expressed in the refined poetics of T.S. Eliot's *Four Quartets* or the crude poetics of Sonny's theatrical preaching, that basic truth of the faith is meant to inspire terror and gratitude. Jesus' earliest followers saw the reversed parallel between Abraham's willingness to butcher his son Isaac in obedience to God and God's willingness to sacrifice his Son for the love of humankind. The more pacific themes of most Christians today mute the terror in favor of the gratitude, but I find the gentler promises of redemption even more disturbing.

The image of children singing "Jesus Loves Me" is repellent to me. It's not just the sentimentality and kitsch. It's the thought of imbuing children with the idea that they are loved, ultimately and unconditionally, only insofar as they accept the Christian faith's story and dogma. The glow of adoration and security which the loving Jesus offers confers on the darkness around it the meaning of abandonment, anomie and punishment. Sin and death are in this sense the fruit of the promise of love and redemption. Children know these things, whether the message comes to them in the fire-and-brimstone shouting of fundamentalists or the reassuring tones of suburban Congregationalists.

ONE OF THE MOST GRUELING QUESTIONS to be faced in raising children without religion is how to approach the question of death. When Sam, my older son, was less than four years old one of his closest friends at pre-school was diagnosed with cancer and died within a few months. Wyatt's illness was a challenge to the school's parents, and we talked anxiously with each other about what we were going to tell our children. Several friends, whose lack of religious beliefs was as pronounced as Jean's and mine, panicked, telling their children that Wyatt wasn't coming to the school anymore or that he had moved to another city or that he was now an angel in heaven. We decided to try to tell Sam about death and give him solace without the fictions. He mulled over our explanations and undoubtedly assessed them against what he saw in many visits to the child who weakened and withered before our eyes. One day as we were coming home, he found a dead butterfly on the porch; he picked it up, sat down and looked at it for a few moments. The butterfly is dead, he told us. We felt he understood more than most adults were willing to. And he mourned in the lower registers of the imagination; standing in front of a mirror the day after his friend died, he declared, I hate Wyatt. I want to eat Wyatt. There was not much sense of triumph in these moments, only relief and hope. How stark can you stand your three-year-old's sense of reality to be?

Deaths often force differences of belief into the open, and they can tear at the closest family bonds. When my sister and I were around thirty, our younger brother, twenty-two, was killed in a motorcycle accident. A few months later she and I drifted into a discussion of religion and the afterlife. She pushed the question: Do you mean you don't believe David is still alive somewhere, in some way? I had to answer, No. Never have I encountered a look of such dismay and accusation, a look with so much packed into it that I didn't know if my words had been for her worse for their hurt or their betrayal or their falsehood.

Between the poignancy of the butterfly and my sister's anguished look lies for me the puzzle of love, belief and death. Believers and nonbelievers ask the same questions, tread the same ground, even as they experience its secular and sacred contours in completely different ways. Families cohere around their shared beliefs, and dissenters can suddenly feel like outsiders. Between parents and children or brothers and sisters or between lovers, differences of belief put tolerance harshly to the test, especially at those moments when there is suffering or loss or wrong that we don't know how to comprehend or bear except through our belief that God is or is not there.

Essay

The world is nothing but an eternal see-saw. Everything in it see-saws incessantly. I am not describing an essence but a transition, an account of various and changeable chance occurrences, of undefined and even, as it happens, contradictory ideas. Not only does the wind of chance bluster me about, but I, in my turn, move and change direction. And anyone who pays close attention to his point of departure will note that he does not arrive at the same location twice.

—Michel de Montaigne

The Pastry Dough of Time: A Meditation on Anachronism

Hans Magnus Enzensberger

THE NOTION OF PROGRESS, as a process of eternal and inexorable perfection, has indeed seen better days. But we continue to speak of "advances" all the same, as they keep on burgeoning, rampant as ever. Progress in this plural form has its devotees, and not only among the agents of the media and advertising. Among scientists, too, and economists, technicians and physicians, progress enjoys an unsullied reputation. In countless little steps it advances ever more quickly in every direction, a process that no one dares steer, let alone seriously question.

While the old political and artistic avant-gardes have abandoned the field, the technological fundamentalists, quite unmoved by the catastrophic experiences of the 20th century, devote themselves without restraint to their visions of the future. Their wide-eyed optimism knows no bounds, not even those of self-preservation. Ultimately their visions are aimed not toward mankind's improvement, but toward the destruction of humanity in order to make way for products that they imagine to be far superior to all biological forms of life. This happy masochism is reminiscent of the time when the splitting of the atom seemed to open up the possibility of a bright future.

But the fundamentalists of the modern age are not the only occupants of the planet. Outside their stringent sects there is a great deal of nervousness. There have always been laggards to hold up the march of progress, but now even the more intelligent business leaders look forward to the promises of technical globalization with rather mixed feelings.

There is a very simple reason for this. With growing rapidity, the number of asynchronisms is also on the rise. Each day progress leaves behind more stragglers in its race toward the future. It has long since left most people in the dust. But it is no longer the case — as it was in the age of the heroic Moderns — of a majority of perpetual slowpokes who would like to deny some self-appointed "avant-garde" their following. Such tidy distinctions are no longer viable. Even the trendsetters get tangled in the most peculiar contradictions. The theorist in artificial intelligence moves into a rehabilitated old building. The weapons expert loves to go to the opera. The deconstructionist suffers the pangs of love, and the microchip designer develops a weakness for the wisdom of Buddha. Of course one could dismiss such inclinations as mere compensation, ripples on the surface. But that can be countered with the argument that these "remnants of the past" seem to proliferate just as uncontrollably as progress. The disowned past expresses itself, against our will and without consideration for our ideological preferences, in a wealth of somatic, psychic and cultural symptoms. That allows for only one conclusion: apparently the time has passed when one could believe in the possibility of an up-to-date life.

THE MUCH VAUNTED POSTMODERNISM was just such a symptom, but it was not capable of grasping the deeper dynamic of asynchronicity. The very term "postmodernism" reveals its own dependence on successive thinking, that scheme in which each epoch follows the last as if on a conveyor belt, only to make way for the next. The central dogma of modernism, enshrined in this shockingly simple image, has withstood all of the shocks and self-doubts of the century.

It is hard to say when and how the idea of succession caught on in the philosophy of history. Perhaps the famous *querelle des anciens et des modernes* of 1687 provides a clue. What began as a struggle between the ancient and modern ages grew into a protracted battle between the inherited past and the revolutionary new, between tradition and the modern, and finally became a given. It has survived into the present as an either/or, first in cultural settings and then in the political arena.

Obviously this was a temptingly persuasive model, because from that time forward everyone could imagine he faced a simple choice. He had only to pick one of two sides — the *ancien régime* or the Revolution, origins or progress, the old Adam or the New Man, right or left — and then he would be equipped with something he could call a worldview or a firm position. Not only have entire intellectual movements worn themselves out with these oppositions, but innumerable millions have paid for their choice with body and soul. Humanity imagined that it faced alternatives of heart-stirring simplicity. The world's incongruities were reduced to a binary system. There seemed to be two and only two options, and from now on one or the other would always lead the way.

When Saint Augustine puzzled, "What is time? If someone asks me, I know; if I have to explain it, I don't," he asked a question for all philosophers. It is an endless meditation in which astrophysicists and cosmologists have also recently begun to take part. As penetrating and complex as most of their theories are, they have not been able to join forces against the most commonplace of all conceptions of time, which takes everything that has happened, is happening and will happen, and places it on a line, with the present functioning as a moveable point that cleanly separates the past from the future. One could almost envy this idea for its simplicity, which leads to such tautologies as "What's past is past." But anyone who embraces this concept of time is defeated immediately by the question of how memory is possible; this simultaneous conjunction of the past and present must be bewildering for such chronologists.

ANACHRONISM, IF ONE DEPENDS UPON GERMAN dictionaries and encyclopedias, is a "violation of the passage of time, of chronology," the "incorrect temporal organization of ideas, things, or people." The English sources express this even more strikingly: "anything done or existing out of date, *hence,* anything which was proper to a former age, but is out of harmony with the present." The accusatory, if not denunciatory, undertone is unmistakable. Woe to the ignoramus who would dare violate the normal passage of time, who organizes his ideas incorrectly or perhaps even does or says something that is *out of date,* out of line with the present. This kind of thing presents an insufferable disturbance to contemporary harmony.

In these definitions a modernist monomania is quite innocently elevated to an objective law. For the person who thinks this way, the rule of the present has become so much a part of nature that he does not even notice it. He behaves as if he could not have a thought or undertake anything without first taking a look at the calendar in order to be sure of what is scheduled. But it is extremely questionable as to whether zombies of this type truly and physically exist. Since the air went out of the historical avant-garde, and not only in the political arena, disc jockeys, lifestyle magazines and multimedia managers are probably the only ones left who take the time signal on the radio seriously.

The modern concept of time runs aground when confronted with the most obvious of data, so obvious it is almost embarrassing to mention it. Our genetic code originated millions and millions of years ago; only a minimal part of it is derived from hominization (the evolutionary period in which humans emerged) and thus represents a relatively late development. Our somatic and psychic equipment is invincibly ancient, to say nothing of what comprises our consciousness. We are composed of layers of time, reaching immeasurably far into the past. Our cultural evolution is just as complex, and in this area, too, the portion of newer elements is relatively small. The "violation of the passage of time," a violation called an exception by the discourse of modernism, is actually the rule. The "new" only skims the thin surface layer of an opaque ocean of latent possibilities. Anachronism is no avoidable mistake, but a fundamental condition of human existence.

TAKE A SQUARE PIECE OF PASTRY DOUGH, fold it over and stretch it so that it is only half as long but twice as wide. Then divide the rectangle in half and lay the right half over the left.

Now begin again from the beginning, stretch the dough a second time, cut it in two and piece the halves together again. This will produce a third square, just as large as the first. Only now it consists of four horizontal strips. Repeat this operation as often as you like.

This process has a cute scientific name. It is called the baker's

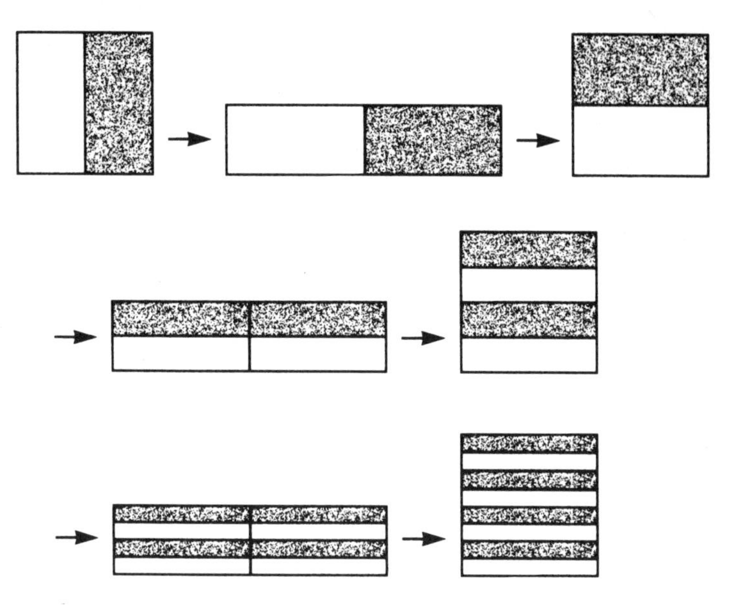

transformation, and its product is a pastry dough of a particularly good quality. With every fourth step the structure becomes more refined. After the tenth time the dough will have reached two to the power of ten layers, and after the twentieth we will have 1,048,576 unimaginably thin layers. Naturally, any baker with an ounce of experience will object that it is impossible to bake a two-dimensional dough. This difficulty is easily set aside. One need only exchange the square for a cube, and the thing would look like this:

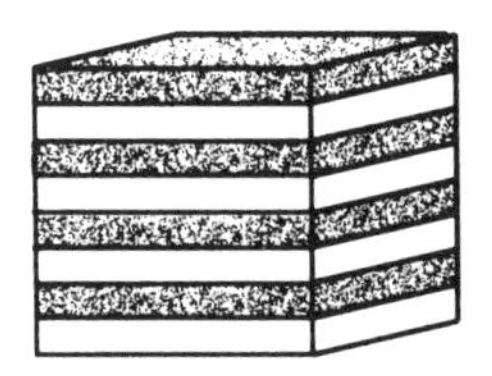

What would happen if we were to apply this simple mathematical model to time or, more precisely and more modestly, to historical time? Just out of curiosity and, if you like, for entertainment, as an alternative to the linear model of time used in classical physics, let's do the experiment. The pastry-dough structure exhibits a number of surprising characteristics that are not immediately apparent. How does any given point behave when the pastry dough is subjected to the baker's transformation. Point A, let's say a granule of sugar or a raisin, wanders back and forth in a bizarre way, like this, for example:

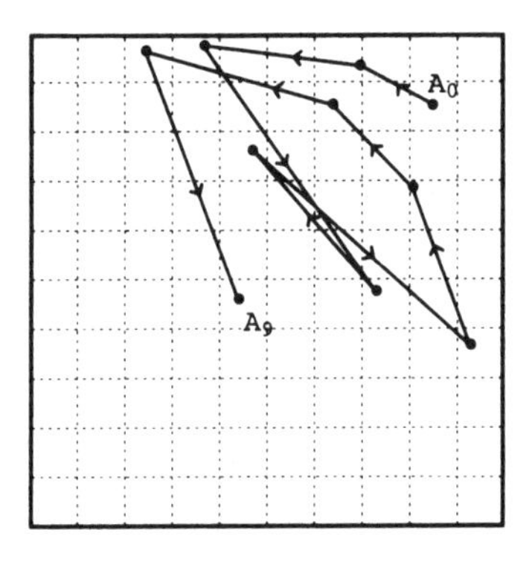

A_0=(0.840675437/0.840675437)

Point B starts out nearby but quickly distances itself from A and blazes a completely different trail:

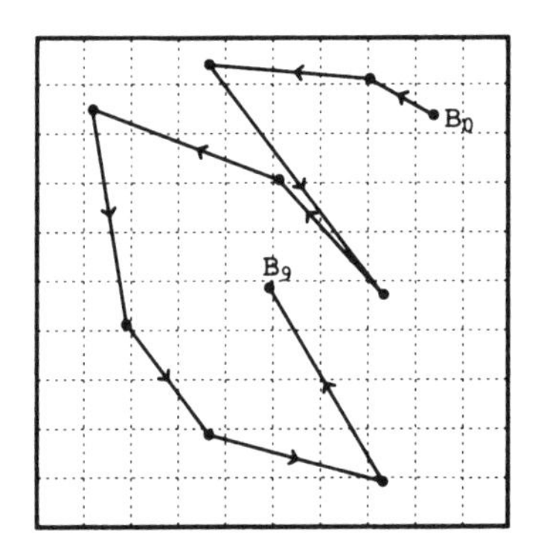

B_0=(0.846704216/0.846704216)

These two trajectories seem accidental, though they were achieved through a strictly deterministic process. If we have all of the original data at our disposal, we can immediately calculate them.

But since we usually do not work in a binary, but rather in a decimal system, we can make it easier on ourselves if we do not divide the dough into two strips with each step, but into ten, from which we can form the respective square each time.

Now, if we specify the length of the side of the original square as 1, we can then define each of its points with two decimal fractions: the first of these coordinates indicates the distance from the y-axis (the left edge), the second from the x-axis (the bottom edge).

A simple trick will now allow us to put aside our pastry dough and simulate the leaps of points A, B, C... with a pocket calculator.

The first point A_0 can be determined with the help of a random number generator: the random key gives us, for example, the values 719260839 and 061492. The corresponding decimal fractions then give us the coordinate A_0: 0.719260839 and 0.061492. It is child's play to use these figures to calculate the journeys taken by our chose point A_0 through every step of the baker's transformation. To do it, we need only take the number from the first decimal place of the first value and put it into the first decimal place of the second. In this way we get each next position:

A:	0.719260839...	0.061492...	(A_0)
	0.19260839...	0.7061492...	(A_1)
	0.9260839...	0.17061492...	(A_2)
	0.260839...	0.917061492...	(A_3)
	0.60839...	0.2917061492...	(A_4)
	0.0839...	0.62917061492...	(A_5)
	0.839...	0.062917061492...	(A_6)
	0.39...	0.8062917061492...	(A_7)

(Mathematicians named this trick the Bernoulli shift after the famous Swiss mathematician who invented it.) On the quadratic plane, the movement of A looks like this:

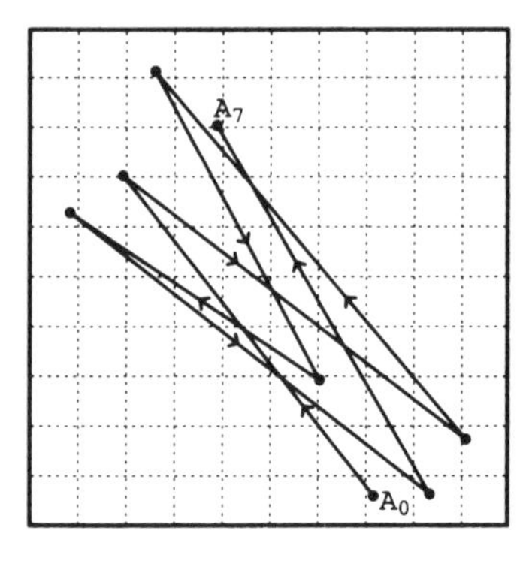

A_0=(0.719260839/0.061492)

If one knows the original coordinates with sufficient precision (whether it is a case of recurring fractions or a chance number with many decimal places after the decimal point), one can continue the game for as long as one wants; that is, one can predict how the points A, B and C will continue to behave on into the future. But what would it look like if one did not know both coordinates but only one them — if there were holes in the information at one's disposal? Then the path of the points seems arbitrary, as in the following examples, and chance takes the place of a calculable occurrence. It becomes impossible for the observer to predict how the individual points will hop back and forth across the plane. (This same paradox, by the way, appears in the operation of the random number generator that gave us the original values; it, too, works with a strictly defined program and nevertheless produces unpredictable values.)

Mathematicians like George Birkhoff, Vladimir Arnold and Stephen Smale have shown that the baker's transformation is no mere form of entertainment but a method upon which many real processes can be modeled, such as theoretical astronomy, the physics of phasic transformations, the dynamics of currents and quantum theory.

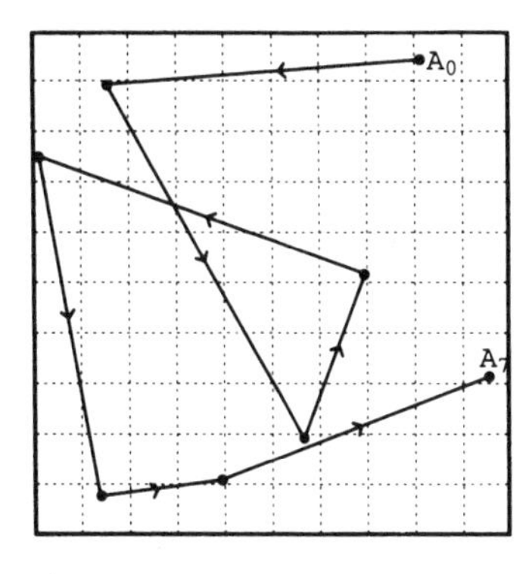

A_0=(0.815701396/0.9453412)

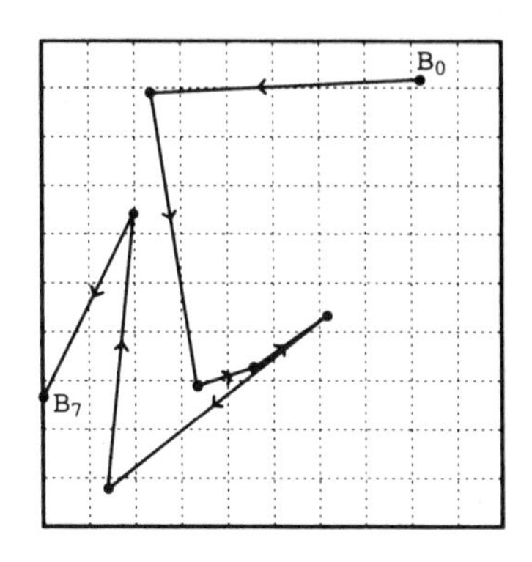

B_0=(0.823462001/0.920311)

PERHAPS IT COULD ALSO BE USED to explain the structure of historical time, its layers and folds, its irritating topology. There, too, we are not able to derive the future from a linearly conceived past. We know from experience that we do not know the consequences of our actions beyond the next step. Extrapolation fails us. Futurology reads coffee grounds. Long-range market and stock forecasters make fools of themselves with their prophecies just as regularly as politicians.

Just as in physical situations, the impossibility of making dependable predictions does not negate the power of causality. Even the unforeseeable is determined; it's just that we never have a complete knowledge of all of the premises — not simply because the past that comes down to us is inevitably incomplete, but in principle.

Our contemporary, baptized in all the waters of modernization, pulls out his hair. Someone is always disturbing the unison of the present, the goodwill of simultaneity. Entire societies behave obdurately. Rather than advancing along the only possible pathway for growth, many of them refuse to get onboard the train of time and follow the advice of the International Monetary Fund. Underdeveloped as they are, they do not want to admit that it is only a matter of time before they will achieve the standards of the United States. On every continent there are stubborn minorities clinging to anachronistic ideas. In order to justify their claims, the incorrigibles refer to battles fought several centuries ago, and they gather hundreds of thousands of followers under medieval-looking banners. No modern achievement is immune from being suddenly dissolved into nothing; there are regions of the world in which even the state has disappeared as an organizing principle. The last word has not even been said on communism. The talk of a dustbin of history, into which the communists wanted to throw their opponents, has turned against them. Now they are the ones who are no longer running in the forefront but are hopelessly to the rear, but still one cannot say with any certainty that this will continue to be so.

But even in the heart of the metropolis the defeat of the outdated does not appear to be fully successful. Superstition, long since unmasked and refuted, has risen again, as if there had never been an Enlightenment. All the things we had settled and disposed of, the great as well as the small, are celebrating their tangled comeback. Furniture that a short time ago would have landed in the dump is now showing up in expensive antique shops. Gregorian chants, which inspired little more than a dismissive shrug of the shoulders scarcely twenty years ago, now have appeared on the music industry's hit charts. There is hardly a motif, no matter how distant and discredited, of which one can be certain that it will not at some point be presented at the costume ball of culture in the radiant attire of sparkling novelty. In short, the "violation of the passage of time, of chronology," is no avoidable accident but an inevitable fact.

IF ONE COULD IMAGINE A STRUCTURE OF HISTORY besides the linear time of classical physics, it might be easier to grasp the leapfrogging of time. In our pastry dough, memory does not exist along a continuum; it is discrete. In the baker's transformation, the dough dissolves into an array of innumerable leaping points which distance themselves from one another in unforeseeable ways, only to meet again, who knows how or when or along what paths. In this way there is an inexhaustibly large number of contacts between different layers of time.

But because this is a dynamic system, there can never be an identical repetition. The leaping point would land exactly in the same place only in the most unlikely case — instead, it will almost always, at least infinitesimally, diverge from its point of origin. Besides that, it will always land in a changed context. Thus the contact between different layers of time does not lead to a return of the same but to an interplay that produces something new each time, something new for both sides. In this sense it is not only the future that is unforeseeable. The past, too, is subject to a continuous change. In the eyes of the observer, who lacks an overview of the entire system, the past is perpetually transformed.

The person who finds this model illuminating will not regard anachronism as a source of irritation but as an essential aspect of a Protean world; instead of denying anachronism, he will find it more rewarding to take account of it and, wherever possible, turn it to productive use. In any case, he will no longer be captive to the illusion that it only takes a mere effort of will to escape the folds in the structure of time.

It is because of time's complex layering that every day surprises us with good and evil, with unexpected advances and setbacks, and that all linear projects, whether progressive or conservative, are sooner or later sabotaged by history. Reactionaries of every description have failed to lead the world back to the conditions of some — more or less imaginary — golden age, and political, technical and cultural revolutions have not been able to eradicate the potential that lies hidden in the enormous pastry dough of time. This stubborn reality has been especially difficult for the engineers of the body and the soul, who can only grasp this reciprocal play of anachronisms as a dull resistance to their unambiguous visions. But it is not only the incurable future-loving reformers who are fixed on linear thinking, but also their opposites, who deal in prognosis on the other side of the looking glass.

The preachers of the apocalypse, too, believe in a perfectly predictable future which allows for no zigzags or anachronism. Their pessimism is just as straight-ahead and unimaginative as the optimism that characterizes the adherents of irresistible progress.

BUT WHAT THE RECIPROCITY between the various layers of historical time actually looks like and what sorts of transformation anachronism produces — these are questions that no formal model can answer. On questions of content, the Bernoulli shift is inadequate, and we must draw on experience.

There is no universal answer, but a collection of microscopic and macroscopic examples could perhaps gives us an initial hint. Some of these cases are as well researched as they are controversial.

The most famous of all anachronisms is the Renaissance. Nobody knows exactly how to date it. Upon closer inspection, the concept unfolds into a plural. We speak of proto-, early, high and late Renaissance; some have even described a Carolingian Renaissance, and finally the term is applied to quite different situations too.

But at the same time, there is no doubt that there were people in Europe who, after centuries characterized by quite different interests, suddenly turned back to antiquity with a terrific energy, reading classical texts, studying their philosophy, imitating their architecture, in a word, connecting to a largely lost, "surpassed" tradition. That such a reciprocal moment took place is not doubted by even the most inveterate revisionists who believe that *the* Renaissance is nothing more than a construct.

Later, every conceivable revivalist movement was given the name "Renaissance," often enough with reference to national traditions, as is the case of the "Irish Renaissance" or the "Catalan Renaissance." In each of these, the "passage of time" is "violated" without a second thought.

While rebirth enjoys primarily a good reputation, atavism is considered a particularly despicable departure from the orderly progression of history. This term, coined by the botanist Hugo de Vries in 1901, was originally meant to describe only "individual regressions to older ancestral conditions." Freed from the biological context, it now serves mostly to brand impulses that resist, more or less violently, the process of modernization. Journalists like to speak in such cases of a regression to darker times, as if ours were perfectly enlightened; the medieval period is usually cited as a dark page of history in this context. Atavism is the opposite, so to speak, of renaissance.

Our judgment of the reciprocity between the old and newer layers of the temporal structure vacillates; on the one hand, we have the recollection of the probable riches of history and, on the other, the fear of barbarism which, although it is difficult to say why, seems to be located in the past.

The temptation to judge anachronism on moral grounds is difficult to resist. But perhaps its actual scandalousness lies precisely in its indifference to such judgments. The pastry dough contains all possibilities, positive as well as negative, in a topological blending that allows for no clear separation.

JUST AS THE LEAPING POINT in the baker's transformation hardly ever returns to its point of origin, the anachronism never quite coincides with the thing it aims for. Instead, it brings out a third thing, something never before seen, in all of the possible steps and forms of transformation, from misunderstanding to reprise, from revision to self-delusion, from productive appropriation to falsification.

For that reason the ever-popular "return to our roots" never achieves its object. The Romantic attachment to the Christian Middle Ages, like all regressive utopias, missed its mark. No one would confuse a neo-Gothic cathedral with one from the 13th century or a Palladian façade with a Roman temple. Every religion has had movements that wanted to turn their backs on the decadent present in order to find their way back to the original purity of their founders. The fundamentalist movements among Christians, Hindus, Jews and Muslims at the end of the 20th century are some of the crassest examples of this. Far from returning to the ancient forms of religious life, they are shot through and through with the crises of Modernism. They would be inconceivable under any other circumstances.

It looks as if misunderstanding is almost a requirement for anachronistic behavior. Projection plays a decisive role. The imaginary portion of renaissance/atavism can be larger or smaller, like the distance between the two points of contact in the pastry dough.

English historians, following the formulation of Eric Hobsbawm, have examined the "invention of tradition," a political practice that bloomed in the 19th century. In order to achieve legitimation, governments and parties, defenders of the status quo and revolutionaries, all came up with far-fetched traditions. Whether it was the coronation ceremony of the British monarch or the popularization of supposedly ancient folk costumes or national martyrs or heroic rebels — the portion of fantasy in all of these cases was significant. And not all of the participants were as honest as the conservative Catholic ideologue Gonzague de

Reynold of Switzerland, who urged his compatriots to "keep up the old traditions and, when necessary, invent them."

From imitation to falsification is just a small step. But even where this line has been crossed, the contact to an older layer of time is the prerequisite for the success of the operation. Every successful swindle has to contain a grain of truth, and so the counterfeiter too must have as exact a knowledge as possible of the past. When the Scot James Macpherson wrote his Ossianic songs, all of Europe was enthralled. The author claimed that his work was a translation from the Gaelic and dated his fictive original back to the third century. For a long time the supposed relic was held to be authentic. This had far-reaching consequences. Macpherson's counterfeit sparked a renaissance in Celtic studies, and the research of Scottish and Irish history owes its essential impulses to him.

When some factions of the 1968 student movement hearkened back to Trotsky's permanent revolution and the Bolshevik idea of the cadre, they launched an unintentional parody, but this same movement helped to bring some buried traditions of the European left to light. Even in its most dubious forms, anachronism can be productive.

It would be reckless to claim this of its most transitory and trivial stages of decline, however, which have appeared in the victory march under the title of postmodernism. Will this costume ball of nostalgia come to an end in the foreseeable future? No one can say. In any case, the industrial-strength reprocessing of the past is a cheerless affair. Retro and recycling are names for strategies of cultural plundering and attrition. But there is no need to get overexcited over this ideological and artistic flea market. Commercial anachronism steers clear of anything truly significant. It would like to replace the leaping point with calculation. It is incapable of discoveries, because it lacks the preparation for conflict, for that "violation" that is the thing that makes the reciprocal relationship with earlier layers in the temporal structure productive in the first place. And so one could speculate that even anachronism has seen better days when it threatens to become anachronistic itself.

BUT THAT WOULD BE GETTING AHEAD OF OURSELVES — an attempt to foresee the unforeseeable, and like every other such attempt, doomed to failure. The unexpected remainder will not allow itself to be driven off under any circumstances. And here I speak, without arrogance, but also without shame, of my own situation. For if there is an anachronistic figure par excellence, it is the poet.

Hardly any other phenomenon has been declared dead as often as this one. Any economist can prove effortlessly that this is a profession which, according to the laws of the market, should not even exist. And as for the media theorists, who have been enthusing for decades about the end of print culture and the death of literature, their number is legion and their joy over simultaneity knows no bounds.

One of the most sensible of them, Jochen Hörisch, compared poetry to paper money: "Both are illusory, both are constructions, both operate in a morally dubious economy of currency and a universal exchange with nearly everything (money makes a product of everything, poetry makes a theme of everything), both are elements of the Gutenberg galaxy, and both will be anachronistic phenomena in the media age." But the terminator does not stop there. He continues with a virtuoso leap: "Or rather, the following prognosis[!] will apply: the future of the (literary) book will depend upon its anachronism — even as regards its external form. Communication will continue to belong to books in the future; information will be in the realm of electronic media."

Up until now the phenomenon of literature has simply blundered on its own hopeless way, "out of harmony with the present," as the dictionary so beautifully put it. Heedless of profitability it shows up in the most unexpected places, an imaginary raisin in the pastry dough, whose future path no one can predict.

Translated from the German by Linda Haverty Rugg

From ZIG ZAG: THE POLITICS OF CULTURE AND VICE VERSA, *by Hans Magnus Enzensberger, to be published by The New Press in November 1998.*

CONTRIBUTORS

Gloria Fisk lives in New York City. "Autobiography of an Escape Artist" is her first published story.

Matthew Stadler's previous novels are *Landscape: Memory, The Dissolution of Nicholas Dee* and *The Sex Offender*. Grove Press is publishing *Allan Stein*. On the staff of *The Stranger* and *Nest*, he lives in Seattle.

Ronit Matalon teaches literature in Tel Aviv. She has published a prize-winning volume of short fiction. Metropolitan Books, Henry Holt and Company, is publishing *The One Facing Us*, her first novel.

Robert Glück is the author of several books, including *Jack the Modernist, Margery Kemp* and *Reader.* His stories have appeared in *Best American Gay Fiction 1996* and *Best American Erotica of 1996*. He teaches creative writing at San Francisco State University.

Stacey D'Erasmo was a Stegner Fellow in Fiction at Stanford University from 1995 to 1997. Her work has appeared in *Boulevard*, the *Voice Literary Supplement* and the anthology *Tasting Life Twice*. She lives in New York City.

Jianying Zha, born and educated in Beijing, lives in Houston. She has published a collection of essays, *China Pop,* in English and a short story collection in Chinese. Her story "Beijing Vanities" appeared in *VENUE* 1.

Alisa Solomon is the author of *Re-dressing the Canon: Essays on Theater and Gender.* She is a reporter and drama critic for the *Village Voice.*

Farah Jasmine Griffin is the author of *"Who Set You Flowin'": The African American Migration Narrative.*

John Brenkman is the author most recently of *Straight Male Modern: A Cultural Critique of Psychoanalysis.*

Hans Magnus Enzensberger, the poet, translator, editor, essayist and dramatist, lives in Berlin. Among recent works available in English are *Political Crumbs, Civil Wars: From L.A. to Bosnia* and *Selected Poems.* "The Pastry Dough of Time" will be included in *Zig Zag: The Politics of Culture and Vice Versa* (The New Press).

Susan Pitocchi is an artist and photographer living in New York City.

World Wide Web Addresses

Additional information is also available through the Publisher's web home page site at http://www.gbhap.com. Full text on-line access and electronic author submissions may also be available.

Ordering information

Four issues per volume. 1997-98 Volume: 1.

Orders may be placed with your usual supplier or at one of the addresses shown below. Claims for nonreceipt of issues will be honored if made within three months of publication of the issue. See Publication Schedule Information. Subscriptions are available for microfilm editions; details will be furnished upon request. All issues are dispatched by airmail throughout the world.

Subscription Rates Base list subscription price (four issues): US $38.00, GB £26.00, ECU 32.00.* This price is available only to individuals whose library subscribes to the journal OR who warrant that the journal is for their own use and provide a home address for mailing. Orders may be sent directly to the Publisher and payment must be made by personal check or credit card.

Separate rates apply to academic and corporate/government institutions. Postage and handling charges are extra.

*ECU (European Currency Unit) is the worldwide base list currency rate; payment can be made by draft drawn on ECU currency at the current conversion rate set by the Publisher. Subscribers should contact their agents or the Publisher. All prices are subject to change without notice.

Publication Schedule Information To ensure your collection is up-to-date, please call the following numbers for information about the latest issue published: 44 (0)118-956-0080 ext. 391; 973-643-7500 ext. 290; or web site: http://www.gbhap.com/reader.htm. Note: If you have a rotary phone, please call our *Customer Service* at the numbers listed below.

Orders should be placed through International Publishers Distributor at one of the addresses below:

IPD Marketing Services, P.O. Box 310, Queen's House, Don Road
St. Helier, Jersey, Channel Islands JE4 OTH
Telephone: 44(0)118-956-0080
Fax: 44(0)118-956-8211

Kent Ridge, PO Box 1180, Singapore 911106, Republic of Singapore
Telephone: 65 741-6933
Fax: 65 741-6922

Yohan Western Publications Distribution Agency, 3-14-9, Okubo, Shinjuku-ku, Tokyo 169, Japan
Telephone: 81 3 3208-0186
Fax: 81 3 3208-5308

P.O. Box 32160, Newark, NJ 07102 USA
Telephone: 1-800-545-8398
Fax: 973-643-7676

Inquiries can also be sent by e-mail: <info@gbhap.com> and the world wide web: http://www.gbhap.com.

This quarterly is sold CIF with title passing to the purchaser at the point of shipment in accordance with the laws of The Netherlands. All claims should be made to your agent or the Publisher.

GENEROUS SUPPORT FOR THE EDITORIAL AND ARTISTIC PREPARATION OF **VENUE** IS PROVIDED BY

WEISSMAN SCHOOL OF ARTS AND SCIENCES,
BERNARD M. BARUCH COLLEGE,
CITY UNIVERSITY OF NEW YORK.
ALEXANDRA W. LOGUE, DEAN.
ROBERT A. PICKEN, ACTING PROVOST.
LOIS S. CRONHOLM, INTERIM PRESIDENT.
